Never in his life had Jason had anyone who depended on him.

He never expected anyone to be there for him, either. After a childhood of aching for a family, he believed he didn't need or want one.

For a long moment he watched the steady rise and fall of baby Max's small chest. When his face wasn't squinched into the color of a pomegranate, the kid sure was sweet looking. Innocent. Special.

His smiles made Jason feel kind of soft inside.

Unable to resist, Jason brought Max against his chest and held his warm little body close. So small. So trusting.

He'd never been this close to a baby. Never held one. He'd never understood why people fussed over them.

But now…

Now he understood.

Dear Reader,

The blissful days of summer may be drawing to a close, but love is just beginning to unfold for six special couples at Special Edition!

This month's THAT'S MY BABY! title is brought to you by reader-favorite Nikki Benjamin. *The Surprise Baby* is a heartfelt marriage of convenience story featuring an aloof CEO whose rigid rules about intimacy—and fatherhood—take a nosedive when an impulsive night of wedded bliss results in a surprise bundle of joy. You won't want to miss this tale about the wondrous power of love.

Fasten your seat belts! In these reunion romances, a trio of lovelorn ladies embark on the rocky road to true love. *The Wedding Ring Promise,* by bestselling author Susan Mallery, features a feisty heroine embarking on the adventure of a lifetime with the gorgeous rebel from her youth. Next, a willful spitfire succumbs to the charms of the tough-talkin' cowboy from her past in *A Family Kind of Guy* by Lisa Jackson—book one in her new FOREVER FAMILY miniseries. And in *Temporary Daddy,* by Jennifer Mikels, an orphaned baby draws an unlikely couple back together—for good!

Also don't miss *Warrior's Woman* by Laurie Paige—a seductive story about the healing force of a tender touch; and forbidden love was never more enticing than when a pair of star-crossed lovers fulfill their true destiny in *Meant To Be Married* by Ruth Wind.

I hope you enjoy each and every story to come!

Sincerely,

Karen Taylor Richman,
Senior Editor

Please address questions and book requests to:
Silhouette Reader Service
U.S.: 3010 Walden Ave., P.O. Box 1325, Buffalo, NY 14269
Canadian: P.O. Box 609, Fort Erie, Ont. L2A 5X3

JENNIFER MIKELS
TEMPORARY DADDY

Published by Silhouette Books
America's Publisher of Contemporary Romance

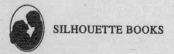

SILHOUETTE BOOKS

RECYCLED PAPER

ISBN 0-373-24192-5

TEMPORARY DADDY

JENNIFER MIKELS

is from Chicago, Illinois, but resides now in Phoenix, Arizona, with her husband, two sons and a shepherd-collie. She enjoys reading, sports, antiques, yard sales and long walks. Though she's done technical writing in public relations, she loves writing romances and happy endings.

CHELSEA'S MEATBALLS

1 lb ground round steak
¼ lb ground pork
1 large potato (cooked and mashed)
2 slices dry toast (crumbled)
1 medium onion (diced)
1 tsp pepper
½ tsp nutmeg
1 tsp salt
1 egg
½ cup cream or milk
½ cup water
1 beef bouillon cube

Combine all ingredients except water and bouillon cube and blend thoroughly. Shape meatballs and brown in nonstick skillet. Then add ½ cup water and a beef bouillon cube and simmer until meatballs are thoroughly cooked.

Makes approximately 50 meatballs, depending on size.

Chapter One

Everyone told her that she had to call him. Chelsea thought a phone call would be the easy part. Seeing Dylan Marek again promised to be more difficult. No woman would look forward to an encounter with a man who'd dumped her for another.

Two years have passed, she reminded herself. If she felt anything now, it was puzzlement. The humiliation had vanished long ago. But she couldn't help wondering what had gone wrong. She could only make assumptions. When he'd asked her out, she'd been thrilled, weak-kneed. Stunned. A man like Dylan, handsome, charming and intelligent, had his choice of women. She'd been euphoric that he'd chosen her.

Small-boned and thin, she'd never been a head-turner. Her mother, her aunt, her cousin, every female in the family, except her, had nice round curves. She supposed she was pretty enough, but nearing thirty, she still looked like someone's kid sister. Despite an oval-shaped face and pretty eyes, freckles foiled any attempt she made at being sexy.

Yet, she was the one he'd chosen. She'd been excited that a man like him was attracted to her. She hadn't thought beyond answering yes to his request to take her to dinner. She'd felt like a princess that first night, but she'd been sure he wouldn't call again. Then he did. He'd taken her to a museum, and lunch at a bistro. Bolder, she'd asked him to go to a family picnic with her. And he'd met Lauren. End of fairy tale. Reality had slammed at her during the following days. He simply stopped calling. The following week he'd shown up at a party with her cousin Lauren draped on his arm.

Chelsea figured if she were given a choice between a croissant or white bread, the croissant would win every time. She'd decided that he'd been bored and had chosen her as a distraction until someone more interesting had caught his eye—namely, her cousin.

"I'd dump something on him when I saw him," her friend and partner, Tess Vanovitch had advised.

Chelsea wasn't vengeful. In fact, a too-forgiving nature ranked as her biggest fault. Because she'd never felt resentment toward Lauren, how could she be angry with him? She simply wished that she'd been spared some embarrassment after his and Lauren's appearance at that party. Mostly, she wished he had chosen her instead of Lauren.

Cheerful and vivacious, Lauren had been fun to be

with. She'd been sweet and understanding and giving. She'd been like a sister to Chelsea, except when a man had been around. More than once, Chelsea had brought one home to meet her parents, and if her cousin arrived, he never called again. She couldn't entirely blame the men. Her cousin flirted openly. And what man wouldn't have been drawn to someone so beautiful?

Because of her love for Lauren, she'd shrugged off hurt about other men. But Dylan had been different. She'd felt something when she was with him, something deeper. She blamed herself for having been hurt by his dismissal. Their relationship had been friendly, but no great love affair.

And now she had to be sensible. It was foolish to think about the past. What had to be done now was more important. Hadn't everyone always said she was sensible? She wore sensible shoes and sensible clothes, had sensible values and attitudes. If someone painted an abstract picture to depict her, they would paint it beige.

Today, they could add a yellow streak, she thought as nervousness skittered through her. Still, she reached for the telephone and punched his phone number. And she prayed that she would think of the right words.

Dylan swore at the sound of the ringing telephone. For the past twenty minutes, he'd sat at the rowing machine and pushed his muscles to the limit. Giving the phone a quick glance, he kept rowing. The answering machine was on; it could record a message.

And he could stay on schedule. He lived by the clock. Timetables, target dates, short- and long-term goals had paved the way to his success.

The phone stopped ringing. But with the sound of a voice, a too-familiar one, he stopped mid-stroke.

"Dylan, it's Chelsea."

Now, there was a name from the past. She'd been tempting. He'd found her shyness refreshing, her wholesome looks pretty, her sweetness enticing. Then he'd realized she was the marrying kind, and he'd run like hell from her.

His curiosity piqued at her calling him after two years, Dylan scrambled off the rower. On the way to the phone, he switched off the stereo, cutting off Bruce Springsteen in mid-note. "Chelsea," he said as he snatched up the receiver. Silence answered him for several seconds, making him wonder if she'd turned chicken and hung up.

"I need to talk to you," she finally said.

She sounded so serious, too serious. "About what?"

"It's too difficult to discuss over the phone," she answered.

The headache he'd awakened with tightened at the back of his neck like a vise. What could she have to say to him that couldn't be said over the phone?

"May I come see you?"

He shouldn't have picked up the phone, he decided. "This isn't a good time for me."

"I need to see you—now," she insisted softly.

She sounded different. The woman he remembered

would hesitate, would take no for an answer without any argument. "What's this about?"

"Really, Dylan—" She paused, revealing a trace of the hesitation, the shyness he recalled in her. "I have to see you," she said, with what sounded like an appeal. "I could be over in fifteen minutes."

In truth, he wanted to see her again, even as he dreaded a face-to-face encounter. He didn't doubt she viewed him as a jerk. Most women classified men that way who promised to call and didn't.

"Dylan?"

Again he heard an edge in her voice. Smart or not, he felt curiosity rise within him once again. "Okay. Come over." Frowning, he set down the receiver. What in the hell would she want to talk to him about after two years? *Why* would she even want to talk to him?

He regretted that they'd never been lovers, never even kissed. Even more, he regretted the way he'd ended seeing her. No explanation, nothing, but he'd viewed that as a smart decision, a safe one. A clean, fast break had meant no second thoughts.

In retrospect, he'd thought seeing her cousin had been the dumbest thing he'd done, but Lauren, beautiful and persuasive, had flattered him with her attentiveness. A free spirit, she had expected nothing from him. That had suited him fine.

Moving toward the bedroom, he rubbed at the back of his neck. He wrote off the headache to jet lag. Next time, he would send someone else when a snag occurred in New Orleans concerning the shipment of building materials. He'd grown weary of hotel rooms,

beds with too-hard or too-soft mattresses and pillows
that required repeated punching yet never cushioned
the head properly. His stomach felt as if some volcano
was erupting, spitting molten lava through it, obviously the result of too many nights eating shrimp jam-
balaya. Good as the food had been, he had simpler
tastes that had him longing for pizza and a beer.

In the bathroom, he brushed away the sweat on his
forehead with the back of his hand, then rummaged
in the medicine cabinet for a bottle of antacid. Still,
he viewed this morning's heartburn as a small price
to pay for success. For the past seventeen years, he'd
climbed the ladder from construction worker to owner
of his own company. At thirty-four, he'd come a long
way from the kid he'd been, who'd belonged nowhere
and who'd had no one.

Rain began before Chelsea backed out of the driveway. The windshield wipers swished, keeping in
rhythm with an old James Taylor song. Music soothed
her—usually. But for the past few moments, she'd
been struggling to keep her spirits high. By nature,
she tried to make the best of difficult situations. But
for the life of her, she couldn't come up with one
uplifting reason for this visit.

Rain was pounding against the car window by the
time she pulled into an uncovered parking lot across
the street from the marble-and-glass condo where Dylan lived. She wouldn't be here now if it wasn't for
Max. Leaning into the back seat, she unfastened him
from his infant seat, then bundled a blanket around
him and snuggled him close.

Belly full from his last bottle, content and sleeping, he was unaware that fate had a unique way of bringing chaos to someone's life, even someone who was only six months old. Lightly, she ran a hand over the back of his dark head, then kissed his soft cheek. Who wouldn't fall in love with this beautiful baby? The sight of his impish smile, the way his eyes sometimes followed her, had melted her heart.

With him close to her breast, she opened the umbrella and braved the downpour. Scurrying toward the building, she battled the onslaught of rain. Even inland from the California coast, the ocean air curled around her, flapping at her wet dress. Behind a sheet of rain, she saw people huddled beneath umbrellas at the corner bus stop. She excused herself as she dashed around one woman, then rushed inside the building.

Her arms drenched, she closed the umbrella with one hand before ambling into the elevator. In its shiny chrome doors, she caught her reflection. Her hair dripped; her soaked flowered dress hung limply. She pushed back wet strands of her reddish blond hair that had escaped the pins. She would really make a great impression.

Cuddled in her arm, Max was bone dry, despite the downpour. As the elevator doors swooshed open, nerves fluttered in her stomach. She'd put off this meeting for a week. During that time, her family had badgered her and Tess had hounded her. Finally the little voice in her head demanded she see him.

So here she was. But if she had any luck at all, Dylan was fat and bald now.

Standing before the door, she pushed the doorbell.

When the door opened, she mentally groaned. She had no luck. Absolutely none.

Unwittingly she felt something slow and explosive detonate within her. He looked wonderful, his skin gleaming. She stared at damp forearms, the dark hair on them glistening.

"I was exercising," he said, indicating he'd traced her stare.

"Hi." Foolish, girlish dreams seemed a breath away when her eyes met his gray ones. He's out of your league, Chelsea, she reminded herself. Even in her teenage years, she'd learned that lesson. The girl next door never captured the eye of the class hunk.

"Chelsea?"

She focused on him, saw that his gaze had drifted to Max.

"Do you want to come in?"

Get a grip, she railed at herself, assuming he'd asked that question once already. Whatever she did, she couldn't let her voice lock.

He sort of smiled, one corner of his mouth lifting. "You look soaked."

Chelsea pushed errant, wet strands back and away from her face. "Yes, it's raining." *Brilliant.* But how could she think clearly? He wore only jeans. Faded to nearly snow white, they encased lean hips and sturdy thighs. Before he caught her, she managed to stop staring at his chest but had already noticed that it was hard and lean and well muscled. She'd never seen this much of him before.

"Did you walk here?" he asked when she passed him in the doorway.

She supposed she looked as if she had. "No." Carefully, she set her wet umbrella on the Mexican tile floor in the foyer. It took effort to meet his stare. His face was one of distinct angles, almost poetic with its straight, aristocratic nose, and a mouth bracketed by deep creases. "I got wet hurrying from my car to the building."

Inwardly she cringed as his eyes swept down her soaked dress. "Sit down. I'll get you a towel."

When he turned away, Chelsea let out a breath she hadn't realized she'd been holding. "Oh, Max," she whispered, and cradled him closer. She hoped this wasn't a mistake, but she didn't have any choice. She had to see him.

Crossing the white carpeting, she skimmed the living room's decor. It was clean, decorated in a palette of whites and grays with a few black accents—the ultimate bachelor pad with a view of Los Angeles and the Pacific Ocean beyond it. Sterile, cold, unwelcoming.

She saw nothing out of place, no cup in the sink, no newspaper folded to the sports page, or a sock tossed on a sofa cushion. A Japanese lacquered plaque and a Japanese screen behind a black-lacquered console were his only concessions to decorations.

"Here you are."

To her relief, he returned wearing a gray T-shirt. It had some saying about men in construction being the best at everything.

"Sit down." Two years ago, he'd done her a favor, Dylan assured himself. She'd married, had a baby.

She had the life she should have, the one he wouldn't give her.

"Would you like coffee?" Whether or not she said yes, he needed it. Settled on one of the charcoal gray chairs, Chelsea looked up from the thick white towel he'd dropped on her lap.

"Yes." Maybe it had been a mistake to come alone. She should have brought reinforcements—her mother or Tess. No, that was something she might have done before. But not now. During the past seven months, she'd become more confident. She'd learned she could do anything she wanted. She could handle difficult situations. Like this one, she hoped.

As he set a cup on the coffee table before her, she kept her head down while she fiddled with Max's blanket.

"It's cute." So was she. He'd seen more beautiful women, but he'd never met one with lovelier eyes. Lake blue framed by dark lashes, they held a person spellbound.

Chelsea forced herself to meet his stare. "It's a he."

He stifled a grin at her affronted look. "Your son is cute."

"My—" Oh, boy. This definitely wasn't going as planned. "His name is Max—Maximillian. And he's not mine."

His grin widened. "I thought—never mind. So how have you been?" Though he'd never been great at small talk, he decided to make a stab at it. Whatever her reason was for seeing him, she obviously hadn't worked up the courage yet to clue him in.

"I'm fine." She was thankful, too, that he wasn't mentioning their past.

"How's your family? Your mother?" *Why are you here?*

"Busy as usual." She'd always found it easier to discuss her family's accomplishments than her own. "She's in charge of several charity fund-raisers."

"And your father?"

The pang, one that came whenever she thought of him, tensed her. "He died seven months ago."

Dylan had met the man at a country club gathering that Lauren had dragged him to. Gray-haired, tall, formidable, Charles Estes Huntsford had swept a critical eye over the room filled with people, leaving Dylan with one impression: the man was a force to be reckoned with. He'd heard that some father-daughter relationships were special, although any kind of family ties remained a mystery to him. But for Chelsea's sake, he offered the expected sympathy. "Sorry."

She merely nodded. She still had difficulty casually discussing her father, but then, even when he'd been alive, she'd never felt comfortable when people had asked her about him.

Vaguely, Dylan recalled a brother. The last date he'd had with her had been at that picnic at her family's estate. To him, picnics had always been beer and hot dogs, not champagne and broiled lobster. She'd introduced him to a throng of people, including her cousin. Rather than mention her, he steered the conversation toward Richman. "What about your brother?"

Richman shined, as usual, Chelsea reflected. He'd

strived for success before he was out of the crib. Her mother always had laughingly said that Richman planned to run the country one day. "He's campaigning for a senate seat."

Dylan took a hearty swallow of coffee. He'd made the polite pleasantries. That wasn't really true. He owed her an apology, an explanation. But after two years that couldn't be why she was here. So what the hell did she want? "Chelsea, why are you here?"

She heard impatience in his voice. Well, her mood wasn't hunky-dory, either. "Because I had no choice."

Dylan sank into a charcoal-colored chair across from her, using the coffee table as a divider. "What is this? A riddle?"

"Did you think I wanted to come?" she asked, sharper than she'd intended. Oh, this wouldn't do. Not at all. She had to be civil, congenial, or she wouldn't get what she wanted. "You didn't ask about Lauren."

Why after all this time would she mention Lauren? "Is that why you're here?" He'd never thought of her as the kind to hold a grudge.

Chelsea curled a hand around Max's bottom. She would do anything for him, even endure this unpleasantness. "Yes, it is."

In the past, he'd always faced difficult moments head-on. A lesson he'd learned in childhood. Pretending everything was okay had only prolonged the inevitable anguish when he'd been told he was going to a different foster home. "What about her?"

Chelsea took a deep breath. Say it, she berated herself. "Lauren and Alan had to go away, so she asked me to watch Max."

A second passed as he registered what she'd said. "The baby is Lauren's?" His eyes darted to the baby, stirring in her embrace, one little hand fisted as he stretched his arm. "You're kidding?" He would never have imagined Lauren as maternal.

Chelsea had forgotten how wonderful his laugh sounded. But this wasn't a laughing matter. She had to do right by Max. "You knew Alan, didn't you? Alan Beemer?"

His replacement in Lauren's life. A man as self-absorbed as she'd been about something he'd never liked—deep-sea diving. "Look, I'm not following you. Why should that matter to me?"

He wasn't making this easy. She could hardly blurt out what she'd come to say. She sipped the strong coffee, now lukewarm, that he'd set before her earlier. "She and Alan went diving for treasures off the African coast." With his stare riveted on her, she drew Max's blanket around him. There was no easy way to tell him. "Lauren and Alan died almost two weeks ago."

"Died? How?" Nearly fifteen months had passed, yet Dylan was shocked that so much could change in the relatively short time since he'd seen Lauren.

Chelsea cuddled Max tighter to her. "There was a storm. According to the authorities, she and Alan didn't heed warnings and bring their boat in."

In disbelief, Dylan shook his head. What a waste. Lauren had always been foolhardy. It seemed she'd met her match in Alan Beemer. No lingering feelings existed for her, but Dylan felt sorrow for the bright-spirited woman who'd lost her life. "I don't know why you were the one to tell me...but thanks for doing it."

Chelsea inhaled deeply. Now was the time. She couldn't put off what she had to say. "There's another reason I'm here."

Dylan didn't consider himself dense. In fact, an above-average intelligence had helped him go from nothing to where he was today. But no matter how hard he tried, he couldn't figure out what else she felt he needed to know.

Shifting, Chelsea fished in her bag for the necessary paper. He would want facts. She would give him one. "This is Max's birth certificate." Chelsea pinched the paper between two fingers and offered it to him. "Please read it," she requested.

For a long moment, Dylan stared at the paper in her hand. There was no reason for her to hand him that, except— An uneasy sensation clenched his stomach. He stretched the distance between them and took the folded paper from her. It stated Father Unknown. *Unknown?*

As he read the paper, Chelsea stared at the crown of his dark head. "Max is yours, isn't he?" she made herself ask. In a split second, a frown of astonishment crept over his face.

In self-defense, he rushed his words. "What is this really about, Chelsea? Are you making this accusation because I left you for Lauren?" he asked, standing. "Is this some sort of vengeance?" The moment the words were out, he regretted them. She was sweet, too sweet to do that.

"Of course not." How could he even think that? Never would she deliberately deceive a man about a child. "This isn't about me. It's about Max. No one knows if he's yours or Alan's," she said, wishing now she hadn't made such a blunt accusation.

"Well, he's not mine." The kid was cute enough. But his? No way. He didn't get himself into this kind of trouble.

Desperately, Chelsea wanted to accept his denial and flee with Max, but in fairness to Max, she couldn't. She had to be certain that Dylan wasn't his father. "How can you be so sure?"

"Because I used protection," he snapped. Straining to stay calm, he said softly, "Only a fool has sex without it."

She would *not* blush, she vowed, but felt the heat of one sweep over her face. "That's not always a guarantee."

That she was right unsettled him. The best birth control methods in the world could fail. "I'm not the father," he repeated. Some other man's spontaneous and impetuous actions had to have produced this baby. "How old is the boy?"

"Max is six months old."

"I haven't seen Lauren in fourteen, almost fifteen months. So let's do some basic math. Pregnancy lasts nine months."

"And six and nine equals fifteen," she said, finished for him. The challenge had slipped out, even surprising her. "Couples sometimes—well, they get together one more time. Then they decide that it really won't work.''

''That didn't happen.''

''Can you prove that?''

He nearly grinned. He wondered when she'd become more sure of herself. What had happened in her life to change her? He doubted he was responsible. More likely an autocratic father no longer influenced her. ''How can anyone prove that? Listen to me.'' He returned to the chair across from her, hunched forward and rested his forearms on his thighs. ''I'm really not his—Max's—father.''

Chelsea took a long swallow of coffee. The bitterness clung to her tongue. Standing, she noticed that Dylan had barely looked at Max.

His head pounding more, Dylan rubbed at tight muscles in the back of his neck. He liked his life uncomplicated—short-term relationships, safe sex without commitment and no emotional ties. Looking up, he saw her and the baby on the way to the door. Let them leave. Oh, damn, how could he? ''Where are you going?''

''I have errands to do.'' She checked her watch and frowned.

In three strides, Dylan crossed to her and blocked her path to the door. He eyed the baby in her arms. Poor kid. He deserved better than this.

As he braked a hairbreadth from her, she felt a flutter spread across her stomach. She'd had her say. Now all she wanted to do was leave with Max.

Before she took a step around him, Dylan held a hand against the door. Deliberately he crowded her, testing himself. A telltale tightness coiled through him. She still unsettled him quicker than any woman he'd ever met. Forget that, he railed at himself. More important is what her goal had been for coming here. Had she wanted him to commit to child support? "You're not dropping this bombshell in my lap and leaving."

Ghosts of the past haunting him, he didn't want this kid eighteen years from now wondering why his old man had deserted him, especially if the remote possibility existed he was that man. "Like you said. How can I be sure?" He studied the baby. He couldn't step away any more than he could step closer. "I need to be sure," he said softly.

Chapter Two

Standing so near her was only intensifying his confusion. Dylan smelled the hint of lavender that was so much a part of her. "How long have you had the baby?"

"Almost a month and a half." Breathing suddenly seemed impossible. He was too close, and she was too tempted to run her fingers along the shadow of the beard darkening his jaw.

"Why do you have him?"

She slipped the straps of her purse to her shoulder. She'd expected these questions before he'd made that quick denial, but now they managed to catch her off guard. "Since my mother was hardly the type to baby-sit, and Aunt Marlin was out of the country, Lauren called me to watch him while she and Alan went to Africa." Max opened his eyes, stared for a moment at her, then gave her one of those smiles that lit up his whole face. "It was not only a favor since Max is a relative, but also a business arrangement."

Dylan tried to make sense of what was happening. "What do you mean a business arrangement?"

Chelsea bent to the side and dug Max's favorite toy, a mirror with colored beads, from the diaper bag. With glee, he awkwardly touched the beads. "I started a new business," she said, holding the toy for Max. When his tiny fingers curled around it, she dug again, this time from a side pocket of her oversize denim shoulder bag and withdrew a business card. "Chores Galore," she announced, handing the card to Dylan.

He stared at the card. "This is your business? You own this company?" He respected her intelligence, but she'd never impressed him as a debutante or the high-powered type. Looking like an earth mother, she stood before him in a scoop-neck, flower-print dress that flowed to her ankles. With the baby in her arms, she appeared, as he'd always imagined her, like a young mother spending time with her child.

"I have a partner." For years, she'd bounced from teaching to culinary classes, to veterinary school. Finding her own niche hadn't been easy, until she'd started a business using skills she'd learned along the way. "We—"

"Who's the partner?" he asked, trying to concentrate on something besides the bundle in her arms.

"Tess Vanovitch. I met her in culinary school. In Paris."

He'd heard from Lauren that she'd gone to Europe,

but her cousin hadn't mentioned Chelsea's fling with cooking.

"I lived there for a while." She had needed to get away from whispers that Chelsea had lost a man to Lauren, yet again.

"You're ringing."

Chelsea shot a look at her purse. While she retrieved her cellular phone, he wandered into the kitchen and yanked open a kitchen drawer. She watched him grab the aspirin bottle, then quickly toss two pills into his mouth. "Chores Galore," she greeted the caller. "Yes, Mr. Farnsworth," she responded, while fanning out Max's blanket.

Mentally she considered her schedule. She would never be able to meet these customers by one o'clock. "Your wife wanted you to remind me that Fluffy is accustomed to a rice-and-egg scramble for breakfast?" She lowered Max to the blanket to give him time to crawl. "No problem, we'll make sure she gets that. Probably Tess will stop in." She said goodbye and finished scribbling notes from the man's last comment about tending to his wife's beloved plants.

Nearby again, Dylan braced a shoulder against the kitchen doorjamb. "A job?"

"A house-sitting job in Bel Air," she offered as an explanation. His eyes were on Max, who'd scooted off the blanket and was tugging at the carpet with chubby little fingers. "Fluffy's the family's Pekingese." Because he continued to be quiet, his eyes intense, she kept talking. "We're the only ones Petrie Farnsworth allows in her home when she's taking a cruise." She stopped rambling, aware he didn't know who she was talking about. Trying not to let him unnerve her, she said. "I have to make a phone call before I leave."

"I'll be back in a few minutes." He took one step away, then shot a look over his shoulder at her. "Don't leave without me," he said firmly before disappearing into the bedroom.

Quickly he stripped off his jeans, then Jockey shorts. In need of the sanctuary of the shower, he reached in and turned on the water. As a kid, he'd focused on taking control of his life. As an adult, he'd taken his own advice, made his own decisions, kept himself free of attachments. Control. That's all he'd cared about. He stepped under the water and groaned at this twist of fate. Now, suddenly, one small baby had that control. What if—what if the boy *was* his?

Chelsea dropped to a sofa cushion and hit the numbers for Tess's home phone number. She definitely wasn't as immune to Dylan as she would have hoped to be. But she meant nothing to him, she reminded herself. Nothing at all. She knew where she stood with him now. Wiser, she wouldn't fall prey to fantasies about them being together.

The click of the phone snapped her from more thoughts. A yawn accompanied Tess's hello.

"I'm glad you're home," Chelsea said.

"Did you call because you want me to go with you?" Tess asked almost immediately.

That would have been a coward's way. Chelsea had known she'd had to face Dylan alone. "I've already gone."

"You've seen him?"

"I'm at his apartment now." On his tummy, Max rose up on his arms and gazed around. "I'm here, sweetie," she said, to reassure him.

"I hope you were talking to Max."

Chelsea rolled her eyes. "Of course I was."

"So are you all right?"

"Nervous," Chelsea admitted. But the worst was over. By avoiding discussion of their past, she'd set ground rules that he seemed willing to comply with. From now on, all she and Dylan had to discuss was Max.

"Has he changed?"

"No. Think business for a minute," Chelsea insisted, not wanting to discuss Dylan when he might overhear them. Quickly she gave Tess the information about the Farnsworths. "Could you house-sit? I'm still busy because of Max."

"What about Max?" Tess asked, switching, too, back to Chelsea's real problem.

Hearing the sound of water running, Chelsea swiftly summarized her meeting with Dylan.

Tess muttered some kind of expletive about the male species. "He's claiming he's not the father? Why are we not surprised?"

"I don't think he's lying."

"Oh-oh. Did he smooth talk you?"

"*He* stopped calling me. Remember?"

"He could be having second thoughts."

Why would he? She'd never measured up to the type of woman he wanted. "He isn't."

Tess was quiet.

"He isn't," Chelsea said more emphatically.

"If you say so. So he doesn't want Max?"

"I told you. He doesn't believe Max is his son. That's entirely different."

"You believe him?"

"Why would he be so adamant about this if he wasn't telling the truth?"

"Need I remind you? Child support can be expensive."

"Dylan's not a liar." Just a man used to women flocking around him, women far more beautiful and sophisticated than her. "But he isn't doing what I thought he would." Her voice trailed off in response to the click of a door opening behind her. "I have to go, Tess."

"Keep me informed," Tess said before Chelsea ended the call.

Dylan strolled toward her in clean jeans and a blue print polo shirt. On the way, he shoved his wallet into his back pocket. His eyes appeared expressionless, giving her no hint of his mood. "Okay, let's go wherever it is you have to go. We can talk this over on the way."

Chelsea gathered Max in her arms. "Dylan, you don't have to go with me," she insisted. "We could arrange a meeting."

What she said made sense, but Dylan didn't feel too sensible right now. He hoped that if he tagged along, then she would say something to ease his uncertainty about the paternity of the baby. "I have time now," he said, opening the door for her.

Outside, under the building's overhang, Dylan paused with Chelsea until she'd opened her umbrella.

In a move too natural to suit her, his hand touched the small of her back. Just showered, he smelled enticingly clean. Determinedly, she ignored the faint tremor in her midsection. Why hadn't it occurred to her that she would have to deal with a resurgence of feelings for him? During the short time they'd been together, she couldn't deny that his smile still warmed her, his eyes still made her feel as if she could lose herself in them.

Dylan stilled as she stopped beside a serviceable-looking van. "This is yours?" he asked, unable to veil his surprise that she'd abandoned her sedate luxury car.

"It's practical." Chelsea unlocked the door, then climbed in with Max. Being with Dylan for any length of time might prove difficult. But she would answer his questions. After that, whatever contact she had with him would be brief and strictly business. Whether or not he proved to be Max's father should be her only concern. Setting Max in his car seat, she tried to see a resemblance between Dylan and him. "Give me a minute to fasten him in his car seat," she said, not looking back.

Dylan stood in the drizzle. She knew about things like that, fastening car seats and feeding babies. He knew zilch. What if the baby was his? How would he care for him? "Doesn't it seem more likely to you that Alan Beemer's his father?" he asked when they settled beside each other inside the van.

Chelsea had seen Alan with Max. He had been affectionate and attentive with him, but she'd never witnessed the loving warmth she would expect a parent to display. "We all thought Max was his, until we saw the birth certificate. Why would Lauren put Unknown for the father's name on the birth certificate?"

He understood her confusion. Someone so honest expected others to act the same way. "How would I know why she'd do something like that?" Dylan said, over the sound of the van engine. "She tended to have a quirky sense of humor and absolutely no common sense. You knew her. She was a free thinker. The last thing she'd do is what was normal."

Over his shoulder, Dylan eyed the boy. Tugging at a miniature stuffed elephant dangling from the side of the car seat, he made sounds that made no sense. The baby had to be Alan Beemer's. But if that were true, then why wasn't his name on the birth certificate? "Why wouldn't Beemer insist she name him as the father?"

At the rare uncertainty in his voice, Chelsea felt a wave of sympathy for him rush through her. "It's possible that Lauren hadn't known which of you really was Max's father," she said as she eased the van into traffic.

For a long moment, Dylan simply stared out the passenger's window. "I don't know anything about taking care of a child." Now, that was an understatement.

Chelsea had hoped he would think this way. But lots of new fathers did. "Did you ever see the movie *Three Men and a Baby?*"

It sounded like a movie about family life. He tended to favor action flicks. "No, why?"

"In the movie, three men get a baby, and they

don't know anything about one." She decided not to mention that each man fell in love with the little girl.

Dylan noticed the rain had stopped. Learning the ABCs of handling a baby had never been one of his goals.

Chelsea negotiated her van onto the driveway of a rambling ranch home. "I'll only be a moment."

"Where are you going?"

"I need to take Waldo for a walk."

Waldo? What kind of name was Waldo? "Who's Waldo?"

"An English sheepdog." She switched off the windshield wipers. "Could you keep an eye on Max?" she asked, and slammed her door before he could protest. Maybe little doses of fatherhood would help him make the decision she knew was best for the baby. Once she didn't have to worry about his claim on Max, then the only hurdle she would face to keeping Max was her aunt.

Swiftly, Dylan rolled down his window. "What's he going to do?"

In mid-stride, Chelsea stopped and smiled back at him. It took effort not to giggle. "Nothing. He's too young to get into trouble."

Slowly, Dylan turned to look at Max's chubby face. He returned a toothless grin. Dylan stared harder. Nope, it wasn't toothless, he realized.

Only a minute or two passed before he heard the sound of a door shutting. Looking out the window, he smiled. A white and black sheepdog galloped beside Chelsea.

As the dog lunged in one direction, yanking the

leash in her hand to its limit, she planted her feet and held firm. "Whoa, Waldo."

Waldo stood as big as a horse. "Need help?" Dylan asked, calling out the window.

Plenty, Chelsea decided. Even Waldo wasn't cooperating today. "Thanks, but I'll manage." Barely. She hoped the lovable dog didn't yank her feet out from under her. "In," she commanded, after opening the back of the van. Tongue hanging, the dog set two front paws inside the van. "Oh, Waldo, come on. You can do it." Bending down, she lifted his hindquarter. For heaving him into the van, she received the reward of his wet tongue across her eyebrow. "You're welcome, Waldo." Winded, she shut the door and rounded the van, then slid behind the steering wheel.

"He's a horse, Chelsea."

"He's adorable," she said, in the dog's defense. "He gets excited when I come because he knows he's going for a walk."

Dylan veiled a grin. She looked frazzled. "What's he got? One tooth?"

Chelsea thought he was losing it. Anyone could see the dog had a full set, plus some razor-sharp fangs. "He has more of course. He's a dog."

"No, not Waldo. Max. He looks as if he has a tooth."

"Yes." She beamed. "Incredible, isn't it?"

"Yeah, it's incredible that he can eat anything with one tooth." He would swear he heard her snort. "Are you laughing at me?"

"No." She pulled a serious face, but humor teetered close to the surface. "You *really* don't know anything about babies, do you."

"Not a thing." He couldn't stop looking at her eyes, sparkling and blue. Hell, he didn't need to notice that or anything else about her.

At the park around the corner, Chelsea coaxed Waldo out of the van while Dylan unloaded the stroller for Max.

"I'll take the leash," he said, slipping it from her fingers in exchange for the stroller. Though he'd never had a dog, walking it felt more natural than pushing a baby's stroller. "Does a kid that age know you're not his mother?" he asked as he let Waldo wander to a tree.

Without warning, Chelsea felt a sadness for Lauren well up inside her. "No, but he knows me. And he's old enough to recognize familiar faces, to lie on his tummy and search for me in a room."

It was clear to Dylan that a connection had been made between her and the baby. For someone like her with a generous heart, she'd had long enough to get attached to the baby. Changing the subject, he asked, "Do you really like running errands for others?"

Chelsea expected talk about Max, not her. "Yes."

Uncertain of what to do about the baby, Dylan needed a few moments to get his head on straight. "Why?"

"I love the variety of the work, planning and catering parties, shopping for gifts, walking dogs, playing nanny." Chelsea bent over and, gathering Max in her arms, settled on a park bench to offer him a bottle.

Dylan let Waldo sniff one more tree, then he sat

beside her. He'd seen other women holding babies, but none had looked more right cradling one in her arms. And she'd definitely bonded with a baby that might be his, one he would have every right to take from her—if he was the father.

"Waldo, down," Chelsea commanded when the dog tugged the leash to its limit. Circling back to her, he plopped on the grass.

Dylan gave her credit. She handled the dog and child with ease.

"Many of our clients are professionals. Usually they're raising a family and want to free their time to spend with their kids."

Pure joy sparkled in her eyes. When he'd started his business, he recalled feeling the same enthusiasm.

"So they have me do the mundane jobs—pick up cleaning, take their car for an emissions test, run their family pet to the vet for its shots." With Max's burp, she set him back in his stroller. "Tess is a financial genius. She handles scheduling and accounting, and we work together on the catering. I prefer the busier work."

"Just the two of you do all the work?" Dylan asked, standing with her to walk back to the van.

"We have one full-time employee. Mrs. Baines. She used to do hospital housekeeping. She's a whiz at dusting and scouring, which is good, because I'm a disaster at organization."

He sent her a puzzled look. She didn't see herself accurately. No one could handle so much and not be organized. He waited until she lifted Max from the stroller, then took charge of maneuvering Waldo back in the van.

"I do all the other jobs, or if we're really busy, a couple of college girls help out." She started to tell him more, but he grinned in a familiar slow, easy way. Her heart hit the wall of her chest with a powerful slam. Please don't look at me like that, don't help me make a fool of myself again. No plea helped. Unbelievably, a slow-moving warmth swept through her.

Oh, she really wished that it had nothing to do with him.

Perhaps she was reacting to the weather. The air was suddenly hotter, stifling. "I have one more stop to make unless you need to get home," she said, welcoming the coolness of the van's air conditioner.

Dylan didn't even know why he'd insisted on coming along. But he accepted that he was as susceptible to her sweetness, to her lack of guile as he'd been before. Squinting against the sudden burst of sunlight glaring in the window, he lowered the visor as she revved the van engine. "I don't." Attached to the visor by a metal clip, a sheet of paper bore a list. Waldo ranked first on it. Dylan scowled at the second notation—wedding invitations. Was there someone in her life now? He gestured at the list. "Are these invitations for you?"

Chelsea backed out of the parking space. She'd hoped Dylan would have grown tired and bored by now. She wasn't so foolish as to believe he was really interested in her life, or her work. This was all inconsequential conversation to him. "They're Tiffany

Meeker's wedding invitations." After she picked them up, she would have to address all two hundred and fifty of them.

The woman's name meant nothing to Dylan.

"A client," she explained.

He'd expected them to be hers. He'd really thought she would be married by now. During his last date with Chelsea at her family's picnic, her cousin Lauren had flirted and chatted about her love for deep-sea fishing, about her need for adventure. "Chelsea talks about you all the time," she'd said. "She's hoping wedding bells will be ringing soon." She'd laughed in that airy way of hers. "I couldn't imagine being tied down, but her main goal in life is a husband and children. That's for other people, not me." It hadn't been one of his goals, either.

Exhausted from his walk, Waldo slept during the drive home. After safely returning him to his owner, Chelsea drove toward the shopping mall.

Dylan saw her concerned glance in Max's direction before she parked. "Want us to stay here?" He'd only volunteered because the kid was sleeping.

"It would help," Chelsea admitted. Though the butterflies in her stomach had calmed, and he hadn't acted as if she were an annoyance he wanted to get rid of, she really needed some breathing space from him.

In the mall, she breezed into the stationery store for the invitations, then dashed back toward the exit. With some satisfaction, she viewed her behavior toward Dylan as acceptable. She hadn't acted like a ninny. She hadn't sounded like some vengeful woman. She'd simply presented the facts.

Returning to the van, she was pleased to see Max still sleeping, his little bow mouth slightly parted. "No problem?"

"None." Except being with her again. Dylan had watched her approach. He'd always liked the way she moved. Back straight, chin up, finishing-school posture. As she raised a hand and fiddled with a pin in her hair, an urge leapt through him to yank all of the pins from her hair, thread his fingers through the soft strands. He'd imagined doing that, and more, with her. Only imagined. He'd never done anything with her.

Chelsea switched on the ignition and glanced at the visor.

"Fifi," Dylan said, having studied the next notation on the list while she'd been gone.

"The Ebhardts' home is nearby. Fifi is their poodle."

"Another walk?"

Why didn't he let her take him home? "You could stay in the car." In fact, she wished he would. The clean, male scent of him had bothered her more than once while they'd been in the close confines of the van.

"I'll go with you." What was the point in backing off now?

With a resigned sigh, Chelsea left the van minutes later to dash toward the front door of a Tudor-style house.

Dylan cursed himself. He must be nuts. The last

woman he had any business getting involved with was her. Trouble. She was definitely trouble for him. He was wrong for her. Why the hell couldn't he remember that?

A squeak from the back seat snapped him around. A feeling close to panic rippled through him. What if the baby started crying?

"Don't want something," he appealed as he saw Max's pudgy face reddening. If he began to wail, what would he do? Dylan grabbed the diaper bag from the back seat and rummaged through it for a toy.

Max's face grew even redder.

"Wait. I'll find something. Don't burst." He closed his hand over a small stuffed frog. "Like this?" he asked, dancing it along the edge of the seat.

Max's eyes fixed on the stuffed animal.

"That's his favorite."

Dylan jerked around to find Chelsea standing beside his open window. "He turned beet red."

She inclined her head toward the back seat to see Max better. "Take a sniff. A good one."

One good inhale, and Dylan curled his lip.

"He needs a diaper change."

"Is that what he was doing?"

Chelsea stifled a smile. "If you would take Fifi, I'll change Max's diaper. Unless you want—"

Dylan guessed her suggestion and pushed open the door. "Give me the dog."

"Okay." Chelsea set Fifi in his arms. "Mrs. Ebhardt is going out soon, so I'm only going to walk Fifi around the block." While she handled the diaper change, he got Max's stroller. When she'd gone to Dylan's apartment this morning, she'd never expected the day to play out this way. She watched him wheel the stroller to her. She doubted he ever expected to be doing that, either.

Dylan almost said as much. "Something doesn't make sense to me." A few moments alone with Max emphasized how much he didn't know, and what a lousy father he would be. "Why isn't he with your aunt?" he asked, handing her Fifi's leash. "She's the baby's grandmother." The one who'd produced the wacky genes Lauren had inherited.

"My aunt has never been very dependable."

Bright-eyed, Max gurgled at a bird singing from his perch on a neighbor's wrought-iron fence.

"Obviously." Dylan set his stride to hers. The sun peeked through the trees, dashing the grass with splashes of light. "But have you contacted her?"

Chelsea pushed the stroller at a pace that wasn't too quick for the small poodle. "I don't know where to find her."

Dylan shoved a hand in the pocket of his jeans and squinted up at the sky. Dark clouds gathered again, shielding part of the sun and promising another downpour. "Doesn't your mother know where her sister is?" He noticed Max was jamming one of the frog's legs in his mouth.

"After she went to Tanzania for the funeral—"

Disbelief settled on his face. "Lauren was buried in Africa?"

"No. She wanted her ashes to fly on the wind over the Indian Ocean." She saw that his frown had deepened. "Aunt Marlin called the family about Lauren's death because she knew I was taking care of Max. She told me where to look for important papers." She stopped the stroller, waiting until Fifi gave up her fascination with one tree. Eagerly, the dog pulled at the leash to wander to the next. "Two days later, Aunt Marlin said she would be in touch again, but in the meantime, would I take care of Max?"

Chelsea looked down as Fifi wrapped the leash around one of her legs. "I know you can't care for Max, but I can."

"Here," Dylan insisted, reaching for the leash.

He moved only a fraction closer, but she felt the heat of him. She couldn't let herself think about him. She was with him because of Max—only because of Max. As Dylan unwound the leash and took control of the dog, Chelsea knew it was time. "As long as the issue of who Max's father is remains questionable, neither I nor any other relative can petition for custody of Max. I want him."

Dylan gave her his full attention. He didn't think he ever heard such conviction in her voice before. She wasn't so wide-eyed, so easily embarrassed or so timid anymore. A confidence emanated from her when she discussed her work, when she talked about Max.

"He's a wonderful baby. But there's a problem," Chelsea said simply. "I thought—" A dozen different thoughts had tumbled through her mind since she'd first entered his apartment. She'd thought he would admit to being Max's father but not want to disrupt his life-style. She'd thought he would be more than willing to let her have Max. She'd thought this would be the one and only time she would see him. And she knew now that wasn't true.

"You thought what?" he asked when they were in the van.

"You need to get a DNA test," she said. "You need to be eliminated as Max's father." Please, she prayed, let him agree.

What he really needed were some quiet moments to analyze this situation. He also needed to talk to his lawyer. For the second time in less than an hour, a feeling close to panic promised to erupt. Dylan stared at the baby. The boy's warm brown eyes were so like Lauren's. His relationship with her had been the brief one of two incompatible people who'd felt an attraction but had had little else in common.

That didn't mean he hadn't felt a warm affection for her. But the boy wasn't his, couldn't be. "I'll go for the test."

Chelsea loosened her death grip on the steering wheel. This was a step in the right direction, wasn't it? The test was necessary to prove he wasn't Max's father. Mentally, she groaned as her real problem slammed at her. She'd foolishly imagined everything going her way, and nothing might. What if the test proved he was Max's father? Far-fetched as it seemed, the possibility existed that he might want to keep Max if he was his son.

Chelsea fretted all the way back to his apartment. Too quiet. Ever since her announcement, he'd been much too quiet to suit her. As she parked, she couldn't stand it any longer. She had to know what he was thinking. "Dylan?"

He'd already stepped out of the car. Holding the door open, he turned his deciphering gaze on her. "Why is all of this so important to you?"

"I told you. No one can adopt him, because you might have rights."

"Adopt him?" Dylan bent forward and rested a forearm on the opened window. She'd surprised him more than once today. "Is that what you want?"

"Yes," she answered, barely able to breathe now that she'd stated her intentions. "I want to adopt him." She'd even seen a lawyer and had adoption papers drawn up.

She'd tossed him a curve. Adopt. She was willing to take on responsibility for another person's child. If only he'd known someone like her when he'd been a kid. "We need to talk some more."

Yes, she knew they did. But going their separate ways for a while was best. "Later."

As she shifted from neutral to drive, Dylan stepped back from the van. "Okay. When will you be back?" He had to ask. If he hadn't, the question would have nagged at him.

Chelsea forced a smile that contradicted the tension coiling within her. She watched his gaze flicker to her lips, felt her heart quicken. Nothing had changed. She still was weak to him. Inwardly, she sighed with annoyance at herself. "I'll call you."

Dylan winced. He'd said those exact words to her two years ago. And had never made the call.

Chapter Three

Unlike him, she was good at her word. At ten the next morning she called. All business, she gave him the name of a lab where she'd taken Max, then hung up. The ball was in Dylan's court now. All he had to do was go to the lab and have blood taken.

A day had passed, and he still hadn't gone. At a job site for the city's new cultural center, Dylan weaved his way past a bulldozer. If the test proved Max belonged to him, what would he do with him? How had his life gone so haywire?

A call from his construction crew foreman turned him around. The success of Marek Construction resulted from his on-the-job vigilance. He would pop in because he left nothing to chance. Almost nothing, he mused, thinking of Max again while he entered the trailer at the job site. He gave himself only a moment, then reached for the telephone and dialed Alex Kellog's phone number.

A second passed before Alex's secretary buzzed his call through.

"Can you pull yourself away from all that legal mumbo jumbo?" Dylan asked. He needed a friend more than a lawyer.

"Need to sweat?"

"Yeah." Dylan didn't offer more explanation. An unspoken understanding existed between them. If a problem plagued either of them, they called the other one and exorcised it on the racquetball court.

"Meet you at the gym at eleven."

Dylan set down the receiver.

Outside the trailer's open door, the grinding of machines and the shouts of men drifted to him. Several of the crew, ready to start their jobs, loitered near the vending machine stocked with sodas. One guy, an old-timer, removed his hard hat and ran his hand over a thin thatch of hair while he laughed with a mixture of amusement and bafflement about his two-year-old grandson.

Edginess crept over Dylan again. How did anyone ever feel easy around someone so small? He could probably master the diaper changing, but parents were guardians, cheerleaders day in and day out—forever. It all sounded mind-boggling.

Swearing softly, he left the trailer, then made his way to his car. Chelsea handled everything efficiently. Chelsea wanted Max. That meant he didn't have to raise him. Even before he finished the thought, his conscience plagued him. He'd been on the other end of that kind of decision. As a child, he'd never understood why he hadn't been wanted. He sure as hell didn't want to make any kid of his live with those same kind of doubts.

Within the hour, sweat was rolling off him. Dylan lunged for the ball, but it flew past him, smacked the wall and bounced off it.

In victory, his friend raised his hands in the air, including the one holding a racket. "Are you done?" he asked between breaths.

"Enough." Winded, Dylan bent over and laid his hands on his knees.

"You played really lousy today." Alex ran a hand over his damp blond hair. "Are you going to tell me now what's bothering you?"

Straightening, Dylan headed for the locker room. "I saw Chelsea. She came to my apartment."

Falling in step with him, Alex tipped his head. Interest flared in his voice. "Why did she come? To slug you?"

She should have, but she'd been pleasant, acting as if the past no longer mattered. Dylan stopped in front of a locker. "Why didn't you ever talk about her?" Alex must have heard gossip. He was a friend of Chelsea and her brother.

Alex opened his locker. "Why didn't you?"

Dylan stripped off his perspiration-soaked T-shirt. "I sort of figured you felt guilty about introducing me to her."

Alex dropped to the bench between the rows of lockers and began unlacing his shoes. "I introduced you because she wanted a room addition built. You're the best in the business. I thought I was doing two friends a favor. I didn't expect you to get taken with her.''

Dylan wiped a towel over his damp face. He didn't bother to deny what had been the truth. The moment he'd walked into her home, he'd felt something he'd never felt anywhere else—warmth. She'd offered him an iced tea. He'd sat at her kitchen table with her, and for the next three hours, they never discussed the job. Though she'd been a bit shy, he'd liked being with her. He'd never met any woman who knew that A. J. Foyt won the Indy 500 four times, that Charlie "Bird" Parker was considered one of the greatest jazz improvisers, who could talk about literature one moment and hockey the next. He'd never known any person so interesting, any woman whose laugh sounded almost musical.

"You never said what went wrong. Why did you walk away from her?"

"I liked her too much."

Thoughtfully, Alex stared at him. They'd been friends for nearly ten years. That was too long for Dylan to hide what was bothering him. "So what's happening now? Why did she come to see you?"

Voices of noontime fitness gurus echoed through the health club. Dylan took a step in the direction of the showers. "Not in a million years would you guess why."

With the wedding invitations only half finished, Chelsea had awakened early to get personal errands out of the way. She expected Dylan's phone call in a few weeks—probably after he received the DNA results.

What she didn't expect when she returned home that afternoon was to find him waiting, sitting on the top step outside her house. Had he come for a reason? Of course he had. He would hardly drop in just to see her.

A nagging headache annoying her, Chelsea climbed the steps toward him. Had he come to tell her that even if Max was his, he would let her adopt him? Or had he come to stop her dream? Maybe he believed he should have custody of Max for now. Illogical. Hadn't he admitted that he knew nothing about babies? "Was there a problem regarding the blood test?" she asked, for that was the only reason she could think of for his visit.

Dylan hadn't missed the surprise that had appeared in her eyes. Wearing a dress and sandals, her hair in a single braid that trailed down her back, she didn't look pleased to see him. He glanced at a sleeping Max in her arms. "No, there wasn't." He thought it best not to tell her that he hadn't gone yet. He wasn't trying to keep anything from her, but how could he explain why he'd put off the blood test when he didn't know the answer? "Will you invite me in?"

No amount of denial would work. Chelsea felt a quick thrill simply because he was there. She fumbled with the house key. "Come in," she said, leaving the door open. "I'll put Max to bed." She was barely in the bedroom when the phone rang. Before it awakened Max, she snatched up the portable phone she'd placed on Max's dresser.

"It's me," Tess said, not offering a greeting. "Did you receive a telephone call from the La Jolla Businesswomen's Society yet?"

Chelsea laid Max gently on the changing table. "Why would I?" she asked, aware of both ebullience and excitement in Tess's voice.

"We've been nominated for Entrepreneur of the Year in a Small Business. That's a mouthful, isn't it?" Tess said on a laugh.

"Tess, don't joke about something like that."

"Who's joking? Chores Galore—us. *We've* been nominated."

Stunned, Chelsea drew a deep breath and repeated what Tess had said. "Really? We've been nominated?" It took effort to keep from squealing, to keep her feet firmly planted when she was mentally flying with joy.

"Are you still breathing?" Tess asked with a laugh.

"Barely." Chelsea couldn't stop smiling.

"Chel?"

She set the receiver between her jaw and shoulder and began changing Max's diaper. "I'm speechless."

"Me, too—almost." Tess laughed again. "Where are you?"

"I'm home. I had to pay the Dawsons' car insurance this morning."

"What finally happened with Dylan?" Tess asked, apparently more interested in Chelsea's personal problem. "Did he ever say he was sorry about being such a jerk two years ago?"

Chelsea couldn't help smiling at Tess's candor. Slim and tall with short raven hair, Tess was always bluntly honest. "No."

More than an apology, Chelsea wished he would have offered an explanation. A pride-saving one that would stop her from believing that he viewed her as too dull. "He's here."

"Where?"

Chelsea finished the diaper change. "At my house."

Tess's silence spoke volumes. Chelsea could imagine her friend's dark eyes clouding with her frown. "He's with you? And where's Max?"

Amusement rose in Chelsea. "Dry and sleeping. In fact, I'm holding him."

"That's okay, then."

"Tess, he's not going to hurt Max."

"Well, maybe not. But you have such a forgiving nature. Don't forget that he's the kind who says 'I'll call you' and doesn't. He dumped you. That's what you said during one of our all-night gab sessions."

Chelsea lowered Max to his crib. Her yakky tendency with her friend might be her downfall one day.

"Remember what happened before."

How could she forget? She hadn't been good enough, pretty enough for him. She needed no reminders. She doubted that she would ever truly trust him again. That didn't mean she'd forgotten what she'd felt when with him, still felt.

Having followed her in, Dylan had waited at the

living room archway. The house, a small brick bungalow in an older part of town, was furnished with a mix of expensive furniture, from a Queen Anne desk to an Early American sofa, as if its occupant's only concern was what pleased her. The rooms felt warm, welcoming, but hardly depicted the life-style of a woman born with a silver spoon in her mouth. A blue-and-white afghan was draped over the arm of a chair, and several potted plants near the front bay window circled one that bore bright reddish orange flowers. Andrew Wyeth artwork adorned the walls.

He wandered to the kitchen doorway and surveyed the room his crew had built at the back of her house. Light poured in through a double sliding glass door, but the room remained unpainted, empty of furniture. Had she been so hurt or hated him so much that she'd abandoned her plan to use it as a home office?

Lured by the sound of her humming, Dylan crossed to what he assumed was a bedroom. In a corner were rolls of wallpaper of dancing Disney characters. He looked past the white dresser to Chelsea standing by the crib, and remained quiet.

A smile playing on her lips, she turned away from the sleeping child and jumped at the sight of him.

"Sorry," Dylan whispered.

Chelsea held a hand to her chest, to her pounding heart. "You're quiet."

"I figured you'd kill me if I woke him."

She strained for a smile. If only she knew why he'd come. At the trill again of the phone, she grimaced, darting a look at Max, then snapped up the receiver.

Not wanting to disturb him, she wandered past Dy-

Ian and into the living room while she listened to the caller's motherly panic. "I can take care of that." She made a note on a sheet of paper before looking at Dylan. "I have to leave."

Here's your hat, what's your hurry? It probably was best he got out of there. He didn't even know why he'd come. "I'll give you a call tomorrow." For a second, her eyes locked with his. Inwardly he cringed. He could tell that he'd reminded her of the last time he'd seen her two years ago. "This time I will," he assured her.

Why didn't you last time? she wanted to ask. Not moving, she watched him leave. He'd gone without telling her why he'd come. Nothing was different, she reminded herself. He still baffled her.

In minutes, she strolled outside with Max in her arms. She was a step from the porch when she saw Dylan. Standing near the back of her van, he was unbolting her spare tire. With effort, she fought the tension within her, the thrill slithering over her.

"You have a flat tire," he said, while rolling the spare tire toward the flat one.

Chelsea trailed him to the right rear tire. As he hunkered down in front of the tire and began loosening lug nuts, muscles rippled in his arms. "Thank you for doing that."

Dylan swiveled a look over his shoulder at her. The afternoon breeze played with a few loosened strands of her hair. "No problem." The frown line between her brows had deepened. He wanted to reach out and touch that line, assure her that he meant her no harm. But how could he? He wasn't convinced himself that wasn't a lie. "You're in a hurry?" he asked, noting she'd checked her watch twice in the past few moments.

"An emergency, of sorts." Chelsea nearly didn't explain, believing someone so successful as he was would view the problem as trivial. "A client's son, Jonathan, forgot his knapsack with a school project in it." Her gaze skimmed the muscles in his arm, which flexed as he pitted them against one stubborn lug nut. "I have to deliver it to him at school."

"How do you get paid for a job like that?"

At his sidelong glance, she managed a flicker of a smile.

"The Hembertsons are regular clients." She set Max in his seat in the back of the van before answering. "I probably won't charge them. Jonathan is such a sweet boy."

Dylan muscled off the last nut and changed the tire. He was going to say something about that being a poor business policy. Instead, he added softhearted to his description of her. Standing, he shot a look at Max in his car seat. "Does he sleep through everything?"

"He's a wonderful baby." Chelsea handed him a paper towel from one of the rolls in the van, then leaned against it. Woozy, she hoped she wasn't getting sick as she recalled a customer yesterday who'd been in bed with flulike symptoms. "He smiles more than he cries."

Dylan finished wiping his hands. He didn't know why he didn't offer her an assurance about Max. He knew she wanted to hear that he wouldn't interfere with her plans to adopt. Something kept him silent.

The possibility still existed that Max was his son. *His son.* Every time he allowed those words to enter his mind, he wasn't sure of what he would do.

"Thanks again." With a hand less steady than she'd expected, Chelsea dug her van keys from the side pocket of her shoulder bag and glanced at her watch once more.

"Will you get there in time?"

"I think so. I promised to get the papers to Jonathan before the lunch break."

And she believed in something he never had—promises. "Since Max is sleeping, do you want me to watch him until you get back?" He realized he'd opened his mouth with a proposition before considering what he might get into, but at the moment, the offer seemed to be the right thing to do.

Slowly, Chelsea angled a look at him. He looked as surprised as she felt about his offer. He also looked as if he regretted it. "Baby-sit? You want to baby-sit?" She found it difficult to believe that he would want to play daddy.

Damn, he didn't know what he wanted, or what he was doing. "It's only for a little while, isn't it?" he asked, uncertain now about his impulsiveness. It was a plunge into fatherhood. Involvement with a capital *I*. The kid and him—alone. But Max was sleeping. As long as he slept, he would be no problem. "You won't be gone long, will you?"

Definitely feeling out-of-sorts, she grabbed at his offer and reached inside the van for Max. "I won't be." Since she would be back in less than an hour, she believed Max would be fine. And by the time she returned, Dylan would recognize what she knew—Max belonged with her. Quickly, she unfastened Max's carrier seat, then whispered, "Be good." Max peeked at her and gave her his sweet smile.

"Is he still asleep?" Dylan asked from behind her.

Chelsea kissed Max's cheek before turning to set Max and his seat in Dylan's arms. "Actually—no." An awake Max, alone with him, made her have second thoughts. "Are you sure you'll be all right with him if I leave?"

Dylan cradled Max and the car seat. Max's brown eyes widened at Dylan. A sleeping baby had seemed like no problem. "What should I do with him?"

Chelsea touched Max's small hand. Maybe this wasn't a good idea, after all. Whenever she'd done anything impulsively, it had come back to haunt her. "He likes it when I sing 'The Wheels of the Truck Go Round and Round.'"

Dylan jerked a look away from the house-key ring that she was slipping on one of his fingers. "You're kidding?"

"No, he really does," she said, deadly serious.

Take him back, Dylan wanted to yell. He didn't even know how to change a diaper. What if the kid needed something else? Like what? he countered. He was six months old. All he needed was that and a bottle. And he noted one of those in the diaper bag she held out to him. Someone capable of the construction of a seven-figure building could muddle his way through an hour with a baby.

"You're sure?" Chelsea asked again, because of

the uncertainty that had flashed in his eyes.

Dylan drummed up a quick smile. "Go."

Before she was even later, she made herself walk away. "Thank you," she called back while rounding the front of the van and climbing into the driver's seat.

Dylan stood for a long moment, watching the van. When it disappeared around the corner, he mentally cursed a twinge of trepidation over the task at hand. After all, what could go wrong? How much trouble could a baby cause? he reasoned.

He soon found out.

He entered the house and settled Max on his tummy on the living room floor. Like Chelsea did, he set toys near Max. The baby showed no interest in anything. His dark eyes rounded and darted around the room, as if searching for Chelsea. A second later, his wail resounded through the rooms. "Don't do that." Dylan dashed around the sofa to pick him up.

Tears flowing down his round cheeks, Max bellowed.

What now? Never in his life had Dylan felt so inept. "Come on, Max," he soothed, picking him up and nestling him against his chest. Gently, Dylan patted his small back with his palm. So small. How could anyone be so small? he wondered. "She'll be right back," he said close to Max's ear, and ambled to the window, then back to the sofa. Max's little mouth quivered with his sobs. Neither the pacing nor rocking stopped the tears. "Wheels go round and round,

round and round.'' Dylan chanted the words four more times.

Max's earsplitting wails answered him.

Chelsea fretted during the drive to the school. What if Max fussed? Did Dylan possess the required patience that an infant sometimes stretched to its limit?

Her head aching, she eased from the car and lumbered toward the school. On the way she quelled anxiety about Max with a reminder that she would be home in minutes.

The noontime job from the panicky client had seemed simple enough, but she wasn't sure what to expect.

Looking feverish, Jonathan was waiting in the nurse's office. Chelsea assisted in contacting his mother, a district attorney, and volunteered to drive Jonathan home where the maid, alerted to his illness, waited. He was sick all the way home. Only a paper bag saved her van seats.

Feeling miserable, too, she ushered him into the house. Before she left him, a wave of nausea hit.

In the van, she swallowed hard. This couldn't be happening to her. She couldn't afford to be sick. She had jobs tomorrow, mostly cooking for Margaret VanHorn's party. And what would she do with Max? She didn't want him to get sick. She didn't want to go near him.

She zipped into the parking lot of a convenience store and took her phone from her purse. Unexpected fatigue weighed her down while she punched out her home phone number. At the click of the phone, she took a moment before responding to Dylan's hello. "Dylan, is Max okay?"

"Where are you?"

"Is he okay?" she insisted, needing that assurance.

"Yeah. Why?"

She would ask him to take Max to her mother's. No, that wouldn't work. Her mother was at a hospital fund-raiser meeting until evening. Tess. Tess would watch Max.

"Chelsea?"

"I feel terrible."

"What do you mean? Terrible? About what?"

Chelsea sagged against the seat. She couldn't call Tess. Today was her wedding anniversary. She'd been looking forward to the special day and evening with her husband. "Sick," she answered. Mrs. Baines loved children. She would watch Max. Scratch that idea, too, she realized instantly. Mrs. Baines had been thrilled the other day because her son was visiting from Florida. There were others she could call. But it would take time. Right now all she wanted to do was plop down somewhere. "Dylan—" She paused, unsure how to form the question. Don't hesitate. Just ask him. "Would you watch Max until I feel better?" Could he? she wondered. She truly doubted he would deal well with wet diapers, spit-up, sticky fingers.

Dylan found the closest chair and jiggled Max in his arms. He'd quieted him once, but his little face squinched with a tearful threat, as if he knew his crying was Dylan's biggest fear. Was this her idea of sweet revenge? "How long?"

"This afternoon." She felt weak, and added, "Perhaps tomorrow." A breakfast of cereal and toast churned in her stomach. "Could you take him home with you?" *Could he do this?* "I don't want him to catch anything."

"Isn't there anyone else who—"

"Yes, I'll try." She swallowed again. "I'll try to get someone. I thought since he might be yours—"

She'd delivered a zinger. "Yeah, yeah, it's no problem." All his life, Dylan had prided himself on never avoiding responsibility. And how could he fault her when all she was doing was protecting the baby? "I can work at home today." Fools act too confident, he reminded himself. An old-time carpenter had offered that warning when he'd been showing Dylan how to use a circular saw.

"Wonderful," she said, with no enthusiasm as her head spun. "There's a Portacrib in the hall closet, and an oversize bag filled with clothes that I keep packed for long hours away from home. The diapers are in the bottom of the linen closet, and you'll find his toys in his room."

"Which toys?" he asked. He needed all the help he could get. The right toys might make a difference.

"Anything, Dylan. He's happy with anything," she said, and swallowed hard against another rise of nausea.

He could do this, Dylan told himself.

"To fix his bottle, just put two scoops of powder in it and fill it with water."

That sounded simple enough to him.

"Have you got a paper and pencil? He has a schedule." She waited a moment, taking several necessary breaths to suppress the sensation crowding her throat, then rattled off feeding and nap times.

A schedule suited Dylan fine. After telling her to feel better—the sooner the better as far as he was concerned—he listened to Chelsea's faint goodbye. It was one thing to watch Max for a short time, but a whole day?

With the sheet of paper in hand, he gathered everything she'd named. He was capable, intelligent. He was bigger than the baby. As long as Max had a schedule, he had no problem doing this.

At seven that evening, Chelsea called, sounding awful. Dylan offered assurances that Max was okay. That wasn't a lie. Dylan had managed more than one diaper change and fed him the bottles according to Chelsea's timetable.

"If you want, I'll call my mother to pick him up," she said between soft breaths.

"No need." Smug, he said goodbye to her. He figured people exaggerated about their difficulties with babies. So far everything had gone according to schedule.

At one that morning, Dylan learned that babies ignored schedules. Max whimpered for a minute or two, then delivered a wake-up call. Dylan fed him a bottle, changed his wet diaper, which offered no other surprises, and muttered soothing words. Nothing stopped Max's discontent.

Rocking Max in his arm, Dylan reached for the telephone, ready to call Chelsea. He'd jabbed at two buttons when an idea hit him. Miraculously, his duet with Bruce Springsteen and dance around the living room worked. Max stopped howling. Even more amazing, within five minutes, his eyes closed.

Never in his life had Dylan had anyone who depended on him. He never expected there to be, or to have someone there for him. After a childhood of aching for a family, he believed he didn't need or want one.

For a long moment, he watched the steady rise and fall of Max's small chest. When his face wasn't squinched and the color of a pomegranate, he sure was sweet looking. Innocent. In a few short hours, Dylan had learned how special he was.

Max had displayed an unbeatable tenaciousness in his efforts to perfect a crawl, had shown a love of anything musical, had delivered smiles that had made Dylan feel kind of soft inside.

Who will you be one day? If Max was his, would he like jazz, play football? More than anything, Dylan had wanted to belong to a team, but joining had made no sense for a kid who never knew where he would be next month, next week, maybe even the next day.

Unable to resist, he brought Max against his chest and held his warm body close. So small. So trusting. He'd never been this close to a baby, never even held one. At one time, he hadn't understood why people fussed over them.

Now he understood.

Instead of lowering Max to the Portacrib, he settled on a chair with him. Lightly, he brushed a finger across the tiny ones. They curled around his, gripping tightly. There was so much he didn't know about him. In fact, he'd never given Max's personal care a second thought. If he learned he was a daddy, he would support him, be around if Max needed him. But where would he live—and who would care for him?

Chapter Four

At nine the next morning, Chelsea inched out of bed on wobbly legs and made her way to the kitchen. With her head no longer pounding, she chanced a cup of tea and a slice of toast. Since her stomach stayed calm, she wrote off last night's misery to some kind of twenty-four-hour bug.

She'd missed Max terribly. Several times during the night, she'd awakened and listened for the sound of Max stirring before she remembered he wasn't there. A sensation, one she could only describe as emptiness, left her physically aching.

Was this the kind of sadness she would feel if Max was taken from her? In weeks, he'd become so much a part of her life that he'd become hers, not Lauren's or Dylan's or some unnamed man's, but hers. Maternal instincts had come naturally to her.

But what about Dylan? she wondered while picking up the telephone receiver. She doubted that children had ever entered the mind of a man who shied from commitments to avoid marriage. How was he faring at fatherhood? Last night, he'd sounded confident. Had he been putting on a good show for her benefit?

She realized that asking Dylan to watch Max could be considered the most manipulative thing she'd ever done in her life. But she hadn't been lying about the flu. She had felt awful. Yet it occurred to her now that the illness might have helped her cause. Dylan had needed to learn firsthand that taking care of a baby wasn't easy. While he might have passed a few hours with Max, he'd needed to fully understand how time-consuming, how demanding a baby was. After a day of playing temporary daddy, even if Dylan was Max's father, he would acknowledge that Max belonged with her, wouldn't he?

The phone rang only twice before Dylan answered, sounding groggy, his voice huskier with sleepiness.

"How are you feeling?"

"Much better," Chelsea answered. As a test of sorts, she took another sip of tea and felt no unsteadiness in her stomach. "Did you have any problems?"

"None," he answered on a yawn, and stretched out his legs on the sofa, keeping Max cradled against his chest.

Chelsea glared at the receiver. How was that possible? Bachelors were supposed to be all thumbs around babies. How could someone so inexperienced with babies get through all those hours without any trouble? "That's good."

"So are you still sick?"

"No." Perhaps he was impatient for her to pick up Max.

"I'm feeling better. I'll come and get him."

"Don't hurry."

"Don't hurry?" Her spirits drooped when she realized he was so capably handling Max. That wasn't what she'd expected him to say. He was supposed to be unnerved, on edge until she came for Max. He wasn't supposed to feel this calm while caring for Max. *Oh, Max, sweet Max. Couldn't you have been difficult just this once?*

"So come when it's convenient for you."

Chelsea sighed. "Okay."

Dylan dropped the receiver in its cradle and plopped his head back on the arm of the sofa. He'd had a total of four hours' sleep. One thing had been evident last night. Max had missed Chelsea. Still did.

As Max whimpered, Dylan patted his back gently. "She'll be here soon. Come on, Max. I'm one of the good guys. Give me a break."

He sure hoped that she hurried.

Within half an hour, Chelsea stood at his door, ringing his doorbell. From the other side, Bruce Springsteen wailed out a popular song.

The music blasted at her when Dylan opened the door. Unshaven, hair mussed, he wore only a pair of jeans. Even with Max nestled against him, he looked rough-edged, more like one of his construction crew than a self-made success story. By Max's red-rimmed eyes, she guessed he'd treated Dylan to a few ear-piercing shrills. Dressed in a buttoned shirt and the denim shorts she'd packed in a bag, he seemed content now, his little finger touching the tip of Dylan's nose. "Thank you for helping with Max," she said over the music.

"No problem." Because she wore dresses that hung to her ankles, he'd never seen her legs. Slender, encased in snug, worn jeans, they stretched forever.

"I usually don't ask strangers for help, but it was an emergency."

Dylan scowled at her back as she passed by him in the doorway. A stranger? Was that how she thought of him now? "We did all right. He didn't like that wheel song." Crossing the room, he switched off the stereo. "But he liked Springsteen."

Chelsea felt a smile stirring. "Usually I hum something more soothing, like the Brahms lullaby."

"Dull, Chelsea," he teased, deciding not to get bent out of shape by her previous comment.

Dull Chelsea. He'd proved that was his opinion of her two years ago. As if he'd been doing it since Max was born, Dylan positioned the nipple of a bottle into Max's eager mouth. She felt a trace of panic. Why had she done this? They looked so comfortable, so natural together. If they got too close, if Dylan was his father, then— She heaved a sigh. That would be wonderful. There was nothing more she could want for Max than to be loved by his father.

"Hey?" Dylan had watched her eyes grow distant as if her mind had wandered elsewhere. "I was joking."

She gave him a slip of a smile, but felt unsettled with her contradictory thoughts. She wanted too much for Max, she realized. She wished for him to have a father, but if Dylan was it, if he bonded with Max, then she would have to let him go. She would lose the baby she loved.

As Max noisily slurped at the bottle, Dylan grinned at him. "Do you want to feed him?"

She desperately needed to hold him. "Yes." The exchange of the bottle was simple enough, but his fingers brushed the soft swell of her breast. Warmth penetrated all the way to her toes. For an instant, only one, she wished that hadn't been an accident. Cuddling Max, she pressed a kiss to his cheek and took in an easily identifiable odor. "You play poker, don't you?"

Dylan cast a crooked grin at her. "When I have time."

She saw the humor in his eyes. "And you play it well."

"I've been known to." Amusement laced his voice now.

"I'm sure of it." Chelsea laughed to lighten her own tense mood. "That's why I'm holding him now and not you."

She warmed a room with her smile, he acknowledged, not for the first time.

"Coward," she chided lightly while digging a diaper from the bag. "You knew it was time for a diaper change."

"Guilty," he admitted, and chuckled. Her good nature had always appealed to him. Perching on the arm of the sofa, he watched them. In a soft, soothing tone, she talked to Max while she pulled off the denim shorts. Legs wiggling, he gave her that nearly tooth-less grin and gurgled repeatedly as if whatever he had to say to her was vital. Dylan caught a repugnant smell as she undid the diaper, and retreated to the bedroom for his shoes.

In seconds, he returned, scanning the living room for his missing sneakers. Done diapering, she was opening his refrigerator. Bent over, she offered him a tantalizing view of her backside. "Looking for some-thing?"

"If I was, I wouldn't find it here." Chelsea eyed the moldy cheese, shriveled cucumber, a few instant lunch packages, beer cans and a bottle of champagne. More bottles, mostly condiments, occupied the shelves. "There's nothing here for him to eat." Straightening, she angled a frown at him. "Max is going to be hungry soon."

At the moment, Max happily kicked his legs at a mobile attached to the Portacrib.

"What were you going to give him for breakfast?" she asked, letting the refrigerator door close.

Dylan couldn't fathom what the problem was. "He's only got one tooth. I didn't think he ate."

"You didn't...?" She burst into laughter.

The musical sound warmed Dylan. She had a great laugh, quick and infectious.

"I'm glad I got here this morning."

Ditto, he mused. She had no idea how much he'd been hoping that she was feeling better.

As he returned her smile, Chelsea felt a flutter in her chest. Of all the men she'd known, he was the only one she'd ever felt connected to. In retrospect, that seemed silly. She'd known others longer, but she'd been so sure he was the one. The foolish, youthful thinking of a romantic, she knew now.

"So what can he eat?"

She pivoted toward the cupboard. *Keep your mind on why you're really with him.* "He can eat cereal, applesauce, bananas. All you have is soup." Chili, too, she noted.

"I eat out," Dylan said as an excuse, wishing he could hear her laugh again. Staring at Max's chubby face and his one tooth, he asked the obvious, "He can really eat a banana?"

"Pureed baby food," Chelsea answered. "But you have no food. I'm going to run to the corner." She needed to get away, put some distance between them, think clearly, mostly remember what had happened in the past. Too often since she'd arrived, she'd felt herself softening toward him. "I noticed there's a little grocery market there."

"I'll go." Dylan headed for the bedroom before she could respond. He needed to get out of his own apartment. He was beginning to wonder if he'd made a mistake two years ago.

Chelsea lounged against the kitchen counter. She'd tried to prevent old feelings from surfacing, but she'd always worn her emotions. Denial was useless. He was the man she'd wanted before. The man she wanted now.

He reappeared, tugging a T-shirt over his head. As he popped his head through the shirt opening, she gestured toward what looked like a blueprint spread out on a corner desk. "You have work to do."

"It can wait." Now, there was a statement he'd thought he would never utter. "And I won't get anything done if he's hungry," he said, ambling to his desk.

Chelsea quelled a grin at his telltale comment, and made a guess. "It wasn't so easy yesterday?"

Dylan withdrew a pad of paper and a pencil from a desk drawer. He saw no point in lying. "He's a tough customer to satisfy."

"I—" She couldn't go on and not tell him the truth. "I really was sick yesterday."

Dylan handed her the paper and pencil. "Here." A grin tugged at the corners of his lips. "I believe you." A yearning swept over him to kiss her, find out what he'd missed two years ago. "Write down what you want me to buy." He really was noticing too much. Her scent, the softness of her hair, even her hands. He'd had a brief relationship with a concert pianist who had such slender fingers and also wore only clear nail polish. Within a week, they'd mutually called it quits, aware opposites might attract but didn't blend. Neither would he and Chelsea.

Honesty ranked high on Chelsea's list of admirable traits. She'd always tried to be fair to people, which she assumed was why her conscience bothered her so much this morning. She hadn't been straight with him about yesterday, not really. "I could have made other arrangements yesterday," she admitted, "but I guess—well, I guess I really wanted you to watch him, to have a difficult time and to realize he needs me, but you did so well."

"He needs you." From across the room, Dylan

eyed his sneakers half hidden under the sofa. "Every time he realized you weren't here, the water works started."

Chelsea laughed softly, pleased. "Really?"

Dylan wiggled his feet into his sneakers. "He hasn't cried since you came in, has he?" Bent over, he tied the shoelaces. "Now, tell me what to buy."

Chelsea handed him the sheet of paper. "You only need to get a few things."

Dylan skimmed the list that would have earned her an A in penmanship. "Be back in a few moments."

The instant the door closed behind him, Chelsea exhaled a long, calming breath. Though nothing had happened between them during the past few moments, her heart thudded hard against her ribs. Tenderly, she traced a fingertip across Max's cheek. She had to remember that they were only together because of Max.

Waiting for Dylan's return, she knelt on the carpet beside Max and sang several songs to him. His attention waning, she hopped his stuffed frog across the carpet in front of him. Again his interest ebbed.

A game of her giving a toy and him ignoring it ensued before colored plastic beads grabbed his attention. While he awkwardly fingered them, she scribbled a list of groceries needed for the VanHorn catering job.

It took effort to concentrate. Even before she'd arrived at Dylan's apartment, she'd given herself some sound advice. She needed to maintain a casual but friendly and definitely business-only relationship with him.

Hearing the door open, she tucked her grocery list

in the side pocket of her shoulder bag. "I thought you would never get back," she said, feeling testy for no real reason.

Dylan angled a look at her. The trip to the market had included a lady who jammed the wheel of her grocery cart at the back of his foot, an antiquated cash register that ran out of tape and a man bending the checker's ear with a complaint about the price of grapes. Taking a moment to keep from snapping at her, he reminded himself that none of this was easy for her, either. "Is he fussy?"

"No." Chelsea sighed and softened her tone. "Not yet." Joining him at the kitchen counter, she offered an apologetic look.

Dylan shrugged. Words weren't necessary. They were both on edge. And he figured he owed her a hell of a lot more apologies than she ever would owe him.

Grateful he let her breeze over her mood, Chelsea lifted a white fast-food bag from the plastic grocery bag. "What's this?"

Dylan sidled closer. "I stopped at a fast-food restaurant on the way back from the market."

From his tummy position on the floor, Max gurgled at him.

Dylan grinned. "Does that mean he recognized me?"

He sounded so pleased. "It doesn't take long. Babies respond to tenderness."

He started to smile, wondering how anyone could be any other way with someone so small, then stopped himself. He couldn't afford to get too taken with either of them. He might want Chelsea, and he would admit he cared what happened to the boy, but people didn't stay in his life. Years ago, he'd learned that lesson. Shoving a hand in the fast-food bag, he withdrew a hamburger, then took a hearty bite. "I bought an extra one for you," he mumbled.

"A hamburger?" Disdainfully, Chelsea eyed the grease-stained paper in his hand. "You're having a hamburger for breakfast?"

"Why not?" He prided himself on a program of good health; he ate right and exercised daily but couldn't resist his share of fast food.

"That's not a good breakfast," she said while opening a cupboard. "Where are the bowls?"

Dylan grinned at her back. She'd delivered the words like some prim-and-proper schoolmarm in an old western movie. He moved behind her to reach into a cupboard. "Here." If he were smart, he would give her a wide berth. She made him feel too damn much. That was the real attraction, he knew. He noticed things, the sunlight on her hair, the smell of her fragrance, the way her voice softened whenever she talked to Max. He'd never been that aware of another woman.

Only a second passed, but time ticked by slowly. Trapped by his arm, Chelsea felt his breath fanning her face and experienced an undeniable jolt of pleasure. She always felt too much, made too much of the simplest actions.

At the sound of Max's babbling, she dug into the bag for the instant oatmeal and went to the sink for water. She noticed Dylan had remembered what she'd forgotten to include on the grocery list and had bought a small carton of milk for the oatmeal. "Do you know that your sink doesn't drain?" she asked, scowling at the slow-draining water.

Dylan poured two cups of coffee, which Chelsea had thoughtfully brewed during his shopping trip, then set one of the cups on the table for her. "It does, but slowly." Straddling a chair, he looked up from the dark brew in his cup to see her moving easily around his kitchen. He'd never invited any woman to his apartment. He took them to dinner, then home. He spent the night with a woman at her place, but never stayed for breakfast, never let himself play out this kind of domestic scene with any of them.

In response to the *ding* of the microwave, Chelsea retrieved the bowl, then lifted Max to his carrier seat and set him in it on a chair across from her. Her legs bordered the seat to keep it secure. The room darkened slightly, signaling that the sun had slipped behind a cloud. Chelsea frowned in the direction of the window. "Did it look as if it would rain?"

Dylan sipped his coffee. A few drops had dotted his car window while he'd waited in the fast-food restaurant's take-out lane. "Think so. Why?"

"Tess and I are catering a garden party the day after tomorrow. I hope the weather clears up by then."

"What happens if it rains?"

She blew at the bowl of cereal. "I've considered that."

He'd expected as much.

"We'll have to move the party inside, but it won't

be as nice. And we wanted to make a good impression."

Fascinated, Dylan watched Max. In anticipation, his mouth opened for the cereal before the spoon touched his lips. "How does your family feel about you doing this line of work?"

More interested in Dylan, Max turned away from the spoon at an untimely moment.

"Maybe disappointed." Chelsea scraped oatmeal from Max's cheek. "If my father had still been alive, he'd have ranted that it was unacceptable for a Huntsford." She wasn't even sure she would have started the business against his wishes. "What about your father?" She couldn't recall Dylan even mentioning him or his family. "Was he in construction?"

"I never knew him," he said flatly.

Chelsea debated with herself about asking more. "If I've made you uncomfortable—"

Dylan silenced her by raising a halting hand. No wonder she was so susceptible to hurt. Don't feel so much for others, he wanted to say. It's safer. "Unlike Max, I knew who he was. He didn't want to know me. He was married, I guess."

From personal experience, from a father so cold he never even hugged her, she knew the cutting power of rejection. As similar as their childhood pain was, they differed in how they'd reacted. He kept himself distanced from people, while she reached out to them. It had caused her heartbreak more than once. Any rejection opened youthful wounds, but to shut out others had never occurred to her. "This is so good, isn't it?" she murmured to Max.

Dylan offered his opinion. "Looks like wallpaper paste."

Chelsea cast an amused smile at him. "Fortunately he's too young to understand you." She dabbed a napkin at Max's mouth. "How did you learn everything to get your business going?"

"When I started working in construction, I was a kid, seventeen. Old-timers got an ego boost when I asked questions. So they'd tell me more." He recalled years of having nothing. He'd rented a room in another guy's garage, taking showers at a YMCA, plunking every dime not needed for survival in a savings account. "It took hard work." He recalled days when blistered hands screamed and muscles burned. It hadn't taken long before those same muscles had strengthened, and calluses had formed on his hands.

As Chelsea slipped a spoon of applesauce into Max's mouth, he babbled with enthusiasm. "Like that, don't you?"

Thoughtfully, Dylan watched them. Was this what it was like to have a wife and a child? Quiet serenity. "I lucked in," he admitted. "The crew foreman liked me. He nudged me into a carpenter's apprentice job, loaned me money for a union card. About seven years later, I heard about someone selling off his equipment."

Chelsea listened intently. They'd discussed likes and dislikes before, but he'd never said so much about his past.

"Then I got a small job, hired a few guys, heavy machinery operators. We built a garage for a man who owned several fast-food restaurants. He gave me the job to build a new one.''

"Ah, now I understand your affinity for junk food,'' she teased.

He warmed. He'd seen a glimpse of this easy manner the last time before he'd been a jerk. "We did the job in record time and under everyone else's bid. Word got around and more business came my way.''

"You make it sound simple, but I know it isn't.'' The sound of rain on the window drew her eyes toward it.

"It was raining the day we met,'' Dylan said, cradling his cup in his hand.

She remembered, too. She'd lost all sensibility about him. To the casual observer, they'd seemed unsuitable. She'd come from old money where men never developed calluses. He'd been all muscle. Gorgeous. She'd felt like those women in that soda commercial ogling a perfect male specimen, her mouth slack, her heart pounding, fantasies blooming. "Are you and Alex still friends?''

"Still are. I saw him yesterday morning. He said hi.'' As his lawyer, Alex had said a lot more when Dylan had told him about her arriving at his door with Max.

"I felt overwhelmed that you and not some workman came about the job.''

Dylan's shoulders moved with his silent laugh. Alex had played on his sympathies. This woman, sweetest thing he'd ever met, had just left the family home to make it on her own. Would Dylan do him a favor? "Alex made it sound as if you were some young thing struggling to make ends meet."

Chelsea looked up, smiling. "He didn't!"

"Sure did."

She moved to the sink with the dirty bowl. "You must have been furious when you learned my last name was Huntsford."

"No," he answered, then laughed with an admittance. "Well, maybe at first."

Chelsea's heart tripped. It was the first time he'd turned the full force of his smile on her since she'd arrived at his door a few days ago.

"But we're friends. It's okay that he had a laugh at my expense."

And had he had one at her expense?

"Do you still like those old movies?"

He'd remembered. Why would he remember anything she'd told him? "When I get a chance. Do you still like science fiction novels?"

"Addicted."

"Why?" she asked seriously.

"Something totally unrealistic shifts the mind away from everyday problems. What actor was it that you liked so much?" Head bent, he closed one eye as if narrowing in on something written on the floor tile. "Oh, yeah. Clark Gable."

She'd told him that when she'd still believed in fantasies coming true, when she'd thought she'd found the man she could fall in love with. Reminiscing was dangerous, she decided, and picked up Max. Gently she transferred him to his carrier seat. "Dylan, if you're concerned about Max's welfare, there's no need," she blurted out, trying to second-guess what had brought him to her house yesterday. "I take good care of him."

He heard the worry in her voice and regretted that he'd caused it. "I know that," he said softly, standing and moving closer. He sensed she planned to leave. He wasn't ready for that yet. "I doubt if I'd find anyone more conscientious than you." He lightly brushed a knuckle across the splattering of freckles on her nose. "Or caring."

Chelsea's breath caught in her throat. A moment passed. No more. At that moment, his touch wasn't as important as his words. No other compliment from him would have moved her so deeply. *I love Max.* She wanted to tell Dylan that, tell him that she and Max belonged together. "If you let me have him, you won't have to worry about his welfare."

How simple she made it sound. He wished he could walk away, give her what she wanted. But he considered himself too honorable to take the way another man might. "I'll be financially responsible for him, if he's mine." Hard as he tried, Dylan didn't see himself in that small face with its wide, almost toothless grin.

"I have money," Chelsea reminded him. "I can—"

Dylan looked away from Max's large dark eyes that were so much like Lauren's. "If he's mine, I'll take care of him." His eyes narrowing, as if he were trying to see inside her, he shook his head. "But that's not what you're getting at, is it?"

"No. Being a father means commitment." Emotion, hot and passionate, flashed in her eyes.

For an instant, a transformation swept over her face, and only one word came to Dylan's mind—*stunning*.

"You couldn't drop in and out of his life willy-nilly."

Willy-nilly? Now, there was a quaint expression.

"He could be hurt." She snatched up Max's roly-poly toy from the floor. "I'll give him a really stable life, Dylan. I'll give him everything he needs."

And he would mean nothing to Max? Dylan realized. "And what's my part in all this?"

The challenge in his voice unnerved her. She'd thought he would be pleased, but he sounded hurt and annoyed. "I never planned to ask anything from you."

Chapter Five

Dylan realized that trying to understand what he was feeling was impossible. He only knew he didn't like what she was saying. "Then why did you even bother to bring him to me?"

"I told you." Nervous, she moved across the room to pick up another toy. "I need you to relinquish your rights. I thought you would want to."

He should have wanted that. He wandered to a window and stared out it. Hell, he didn't know *what* he wanted.

"There's so much to think about," Chelsea said, to tip the scale her way. "You don't know anything about immunizations and childhood illnesses and—"

Did she think he needed the reminders? "You don't have to go on. I agree. I don't know anything."

"Eighteen years," Chelsea felt compelled to add.

Dylan leaned against the window edge. "What's eighteen years?"

Anxious, Chelsea rounded the sofa and gathered up Max's yellow duck and stuffed rabbit. "You'd be responsible for Max that long." Though she believed a real parent never stopped being there for an offspring.

Dylan knew the way it worked. He'd heard employees talking. PTA meetings, Little League games, school plays, impossible life-styles while they juggled work and child-rearing. He preferred being single, instead of being like many of his friends who were unhappy with their marriage or bitter after a divorce. Family was overrated. He knew it provided more downs than ups in a person's life.

"I believe my aunt will be back soon. So if we do learn you're Max's father, we'll see a lawyer and then—"

Until that moment, he'd always viewed her as pragmatic. "You're assuming she'll let you adopt him, aren't you."

"I'm being logical," she clarified, but she really wasn't as confident as she sounded.

A wry grin curved his lips. "Hardly. You're like the little kid who believes if he wishes for something, it's his." He knew differently. He'd wanted, yearned for a lot of things as a child. Wanting something until you ached didn't matter.

To defend herself, Chelsea squarely faced him. "I am being realistic," she said with as much steadiness as she could muster. "My aunt breezes in and out of town without even a phone call to the family. She's always been adventurous and a world traveler. I doubt she would want to give up her freedom to care for Max." In fact, Chelsea was counting on that once her aunt returned home.

"And what about me?" he asked, wondering if she'd analyzed him so thoroughly.

"Lauren told me years ago you said you didn't want to make any commitments. Has that changed?"

She made him feel as if he should apologize for what he knew was right for him. "No, that hasn't." He hadn't been Chelsea's Prince Charming. He couldn't then—or now—give her all she longed for. But that didn't change the attraction that he felt for her. Beautiful women had breezed in and out of his life. Only when he was with her had he felt that beauty was more than skin deep.

Step away, he warned himself. He meant to. Then he looked at her mouth. Glossy, but bare of lipstick, it invited him. As if it had a will of its own, his hand rose to her face. How easy it would be to pull her closer. He needed to remember why he'd never kissed her. Too young. But she wasn't anymore. Too inexperienced. That might not be true, either. But she was the "forever" kind, the type of woman who only knew one way to love—completely. Then he took a deep breath and drew in the scent of her. Mentally, he cursed himself as he slid his hand to the curve of her waist and brought his mouth a hairbreadth from hers.

Chelsea searched his face. "What—what are you doing?" Was he going to kiss her? Why would he? He hadn't wanted to before. She hadn't changed on the outside. A look in the mirror revealed the same simple face with its light sprinkling of freckles.

Dylan grappled for control not to grab her, but with his other hand, he lightly cupped her chin, forcing her to meet his gaze. ''What I thought about doing two years ago.''

It took a second for her mind to register what he meant. In that second, his mouth closed over hers. Of course, she could have stopped him, could have stepped away. No, she couldn't. His mouth was hot and demanding. It was fulfilling a fantasy. Her lids fluttered as yearning rose within her. Then his tongue traced the line of her lips. When it probed until she parted them, she jerked in his embrace, unprepared for the warm moistness.

Heat rushed over her as she breathed in the taste of him. She leaned even closer to the warmth of his body, heard his low groan. Coiling her arms around his neck, she knew she was feeling too much. But a part of him was inside her. If she felt like this from a kiss, surely she would die if flesh mingled and she allowed herself to become physically intimate with this man.

Eyes closed, she wanted the sensations rippling through her to go on forever. She'd dreamed of touching the back of his neck, feeling the texture of his hair. She'd wondered about the broadness of his shoulders, the muscles in his back. Her fingers skimming over them, she relished the hardness, the strength that made him so male.

Warmth seeped through her. Need sprang alive. Her heart pounding, she felt weak, vulnerable. A sweet pang of longing swept through her to take whatever he offered. She would have played the fool even more thoroughly this time if he'd let her, but slowly, almost reluctantly it seemed, he pulled back. With some satisfaction, she noted that he seemed just as breathless. She was glad. Possibly he, too, had trembled. Perhaps he had felt the need rise within him. But for her, or would any woman do?

Her face warmed as she thought about how she'd clung to him, how she'd kissed him back as if starving for affection. But that wasn't true. She'd never wanted any man like that before now. Though he no longer touched her, she was still aching. She still wanted more.

Her taste lingering on his lips, Dylan silently swore at himself. Why had he even touched her? Why in the hell had he kissed her? Why did she have to be so soft? He'd expected her to be stiff in his arms, not soft and warm and clinging. He'd smelled the scent of lavender, a remembered scent that had haunted him for two years. His blood roared in his head. Later, he would think about that and the passion in her kiss.

Right now he was dealing with the way she looked: Stunned. The dreamy disbelief in her blue eyes emphasized all he'd tried to prevent before. He felt like a Class A jerk for leading her on. He couldn't get involved with her. She belonged behind a white picket fence, nurturing plants, baking bread, having babies. She was exactly the type of woman he'd stayed clear of. But her kiss had exploded something within him. Her honest craving, the intensity of her response had unbalanced him. ''That shouldn't have happened." *Fine time to remember that.* "We need to talk, clear the air."

Her lips tingled; her body felt cold without his heat against her. "About what?"

"About us. About Lauren."

As if cold water had been tossed at her, she straightened her back. "Why are you insisting we talk about that now?" She didn't want to think about anything but the kiss.

"Because you and I have to be together until my role in the baby's life is determined." Dylan exhaled a breath slowly. *Lauren.* The months he'd spent with her had proved he wasn't suited for even short-term commitment. And he sure as hell wasn't husband material.

No longer breathless, Chelsea found herself pulled back in time. "You aren't the first who took one look at Lauren and forgot I existed."

"You sell yourself short," he said, angry she would believe that. Her honest, wholesome quality was far lovelier than Lauren's more sophisticated looks. He'd been suckered in the first time he'd noticed the freckles lightly dusting her nose.

Chelsea saw no point in pretending. "Every male I dated couldn't resist her. They'd meet her and that was that," she said, being up front because he could learn that from anyone.

"They were fools." Especially him. Unwittingly, he'd hurt her deeply. "Lauren and I just happened. She'd been looking for fun and good times." She'd been less complicated. "I'd already stopped dating you when I ran into her at a restaurant."

Chelsea didn't want to know the details. She truly didn't.

Guilt weighed him down. "I'm sorry." Until he'd said those words to her, he hadn't realized how much he'd needed exoneration from her.

"Please, don't." Her pride rushed forward again, demanding she resist any token apology. She didn't want his sympathy or his pity.

"You won't accept my apology, or it doesn't matter?" When she slipped free of his grip, he didn't stop her. What was it that he was really guilty of? "Chelsea, did something else happen?"

"Why did you have to go to my brother's birthday celebration with Lauren that next weekend?"

Dylan frowned, trying to remember the date. Lauren had called him, asked him to go with her. It had been their first date. She'd been wearing a slinky, low-cut red silk. She'd looked great. But he remembered another woman from that night. At one point, he'd met Chelsea's eyes, which were clouded with a sadness that made him want to squirm. She'd looked sweet, lovely in a white gauze-and-lace dress, and her hair pulled back. Twice he'd tried to talk to her, but she'd avoided him.

"Everyone knew," she said quietly, almost matter-of-factly.

"Everyone knew what?"

The embarrassment she'd felt that night drifted over her. "That I'd been dating you. So it was clear to them what happened when you came with Lauren."

Under his breath, Dylan cursed. Everyone had believed that he'd dumped her for her cousin. Damn. How could he have been so stupid, so insensitive? He'd hurt a lovely, sweet woman, someone who probably had never harmed anyone in her whole life. "I didn't mean to hurt you."

Head down, she avoided his stare. If she could have a wish, it would be that the floor would open and let her disappear. "Okay."

Distress for her tensed him. She'd said the word too easily, with too much indifference. "If I'd known—"

"If you had known that I'd always played second fiddle to my cousin, would you have chosen me instead?"

He felt as if he'd been punched in the stomach. No, he wouldn't have. But not for the reason she believed. Unknowingly, he'd caused her a great deal of hurt. More than alleviating his own guilt now, he wanted to ease the memory of a time that had been humiliating to her because of him. But dammit, he didn't know what to say.

Chelsea averted her face, not wanting to meet his eyes, and lifted Max in her arms.

"If you believe nothing else I say to you, know this," Dylan insisted. "I didn't choose her instead of you."

Did he really expect her to believe him? "I should go."

Dylan watched her rush toward the door as if she were running from something.

"Thanks again for watching Max."

"What about all of Max's stuff?" he asked, stalling her from going out that door.

Chelsea turned, but avoided his stare. "I'll be busy tomorrow, and the next day." She surveyed Max's possessions, then swiftly crossed the room and grabbed Max's stuffed teddy bear and the frog. He might miss them. "I'll make arrangements with you to get the rest of this," she said, while sweeping a glance over the Portacrib and the toys strewn on the carpeting.

"I'll bring them by." At the door with her, Dylan reached around her to open it.

Chelsea stared at the hallway, her path to escape. Not knowing Max's future, they had to get along. Sensible Chelsea reigns again, she reflected self-deprecatingly. "Okay, but—"

"But what?" He inclined his head to see her better.

"Don't do that again," she insisted.

Nerves. Dylan heard them in her voice. "Don't do what?"

Trusting carried too high a price—heartbreak. Despite what he'd said about not choosing Lauren instead of her, nothing he ever said would convince her that he hadn't asked her out on a whim. She faced him squarely. He stood so near. With a barely perceptible move, she could have pressed against him. "Don't kiss me again," she said, then brushed past him and stepped into the hallway.

All the way to the airport to pick up a client's relative, she mentally kicked herself. Why had she even mentioned the kiss? What if she'd misread his intentions? Her face warmed with the thought. What if he never planned to kiss her again, and she'd made that assumption? After all, he could have any woman he wanted. Why would he want her?

She wrote off *the* kiss to insanity on her part and some kind of whim on his, and vowed not to allow a too-romantic soul to twist those moments into something memorable.

She wondered how other women learned to say the right things, to be so poised and seductive with men. Though she managed her share of composure in most situations, as far as man-woman relationships were concerned, she was a klutz. She'd never been terribly popular with boys. For years, she'd taken refuge in books.

She thought of her thirteenth year and the torturous hours she'd endured at dance class until her pleading had convinced her mother to let her take harp lessons instead. Her father had thrown a fit. Where would she play the harp? he'd bellowed at Chelsea's mother. Aware of his disapproval, she'd agreed to return to the dance class. Her mother had held firm against him. If her daughter wanted harp lessons instead, then that's what she would take. Later, because of that decision, her mother had blamed herself when Chelsea had been excluded from Lauren's circle of friends. It had been unnecessary blame. Chelsea had chosen to stay clear of them. They had all sparkled, and an ordinary girl like her had felt out of place around such tanned, pretty people. She'd never felt in competition with Lauren, just eclipsed by her.

Maybe she hadn't misread Dylan, she countered. If

that were true, she'd made the right decision. She would never keep her heart safe if she had a physical relationship with him. How rational she sounded now. She always thought clearly when he wasn't around, when his eyes weren't on hers, when he wasn't looking at her as if everything she was saying was interesting.

Wasn't that what had caused her so much disappointment before? He'd made her believe that *he* thought she was special, that *he* could pick any woman he wanted and had chosen her. Had he awakened one morning and wondered if he had been losing his mind to date her?

Growing weary of her own thoughts, she looked up to watch passengers deplane.

By three o'clock, she was stepping into her mother's home for their weekly Wednesday afternoon tea. Usually it meant a pleasant time to play catch-up.

Today, Chelsea arrived to find her mother's friend sitting on the terrace with her. Elizabeth Cumberland loved to gossip.

"Chelsea, how nice to see you again," she said gaily. "And you have Lauren's little one with you." A pear-shaped woman, from her coiffed salt-and-pepper hair to the tips of her designer shoes, Elizabeth emanated affluence. "You have a graciousness so rarely encountered today."

Chelsea nodded a thank you. She didn't want to hear the woman's reason for making such a comment.

Elizabeth was in fine form. She went on without any encouragement. "After all, Lauren—poor dear, dying so young—wasn't always wonderful to you. I recall several times that she flirted with men you brought to parties. Isn't that right, Victoria?'' she said, though she barely glanced at Chelsea's mother.

Petite, with the curves of a woman a decade younger, her mother possessed porcelain good looks that still turned heads. ''I believe you came about the heart foundation fund-raiser,'' she said, trying to side-track Elizabeth.

''Yes, yes. You know, Chelsea, few women your age would forgive and forget. But then, you're seeing that man again, aren't you?''

Chelsea's head snapped up.

''Mrs. Ebhardt said she looked out the window when you took her Fifi for a walk, and she saw him waiting with the baby.'' Her head cocked questioningly. ''He isn't the baby's father, is he? What was his name?''

''Dylan Marek.'' Chelsea breezed past her other question. ''Mrs. Ebhardt loves that dog.''

''Oh, yes, but she gets carried away.'' She swung a look at Chelsea's mother. ''Don't you think so, Victoria? After all, a room of its very own for a dog. It's pink and frilly and looks like a little girl's nursery.'' She shuddered with disapproval. ''Silly woman.''

Her usual tact in place, her mother maneuvered her friend's conversation back to the charity fund-raiser.

Giving them time to talk, Chelsea sat with Max on the manicured lawn beyond the terrace. Placing supporting hands under his arms, she held him until he'd steadied himself in a sitting position. Interested in the grass, he swayed forward to tug at the green blades.

Everything was so new to his inquisitive mind. She wondered if new mothers felt the same joy when their child discovered something new.

"Ta-ta, Chelsea," Elizabeth called out.

Chelsea waved back. "Goodbye, Mrs. Cumberland." Alone with Max, she closed her hands over his. She imagined Elizabeth was drilling her mother with questions about Max, her and Dylan.

"Ah, good, you're here." Richman's crisp tone distracted her from a game of pat-a-cake with Max. He crossed to the table and snatched a tea cake from the silver tray. Tall and lean, her brother was, as always, immaculately dressed. "Did Mother tell you that we're having a small gathering at the beginning of next month for a few contributors to my campaign?"

Tension eased from her body when she realized the focus of the conversation wouldn't be on her.

"Stand up straight. Other girls your age have goals," she recalled her father saying disapprovingly during her awkward teenage years. Not her mother, bless her heart. In her eyes, Chelsea had never done anything wrong. *"Be yourself,"* she'd always said. *"Your sweetness outshines all the others fancied up for the dance."*

But she'd been wrong. At every dance she'd attended during her adolescence, hours had passed with her sitting on a chair, and no one had seen her sweetness. They'd seen a painfully thin girl with reddish blond hair and braces. While Lauren had whirled around the dance floor, her slender fingers cupping in a wave every time she'd waltzed by, no one had asked Chelsea to dance.

"We'll expect you," Richman murmured between bites.

Chelsea abandoned the painful recollection. "Say hello," she teased. He pulled a face, one she'd seen hundreds of times in her youth that made him look twelve again.

Crouching beside her, he laid a gentle hand on the top of Max's head. "I tried to call you earlier," he said, with no annoyance in his voice, "but you're never home."

"I've had a lot of little jobs today."

He heaved an exasperated sigh.

She knew he expected her to tire of the business she'd started. She'd be the first to admit that she'd dabbled with many things in the past. For someone who came from a family of overachievers, she'd been committing an unwritten mortal sin by Huntsford standards. She so desperately wanted this business to succeed, to prove something to her family, but mostly to herself.

Squinting from the glare of the sun, Richman stood up. "I wish you would start acting like yourself again before the election."

Chelsea nearly laughed. Her brother was too young for senility. How could he have forgotten that she never fit the Huntsford image?

"I really thought this new phase of yours would have ended by now."

It amazed her how much he sometimes sounded like her father. He'd always said that to her, too.

"Toilet bowls have to be cleaned," she said lightly. With his moan, she restrained a laugh. "Rich, we have clients you'd approve of, like Mavis Lord's aunt. You don't know her. She moved here from Palm Beach a few weeks ago."

Distress flashed across his face. "You—you didn't tell her your name?"

"She wasn't interested."

"Thank heaven." He shoved a hand in his pants pocket. "I don't want to imagine what the media might do. The very idea of a United States senator's sister scrubbing floors for a living would—"

"You aren't senator yet."

"A mere technicality."

His confidence always amazed her. "Voting is a mere technicality?"

"It will be," he said, with all the assurance that came from someone who'd never been refused anything all his life.

Chelsea looked away as Max wailed about his dropped pacifier.

Shifting his focus to Max, her brother frowned. "Isn't Marek back from his trip yet?"

"He's home." Deliberately, she hadn't shared with him her plans to adopt Max. "But there's been a slight complication."

His frown deepened, knitting his brows. "But you will handle this situation soon, won't you?"

She dug a clean pacifier from the diaper bag and offered it to Max. "Yes."

"Richman, I didn't expect you." Victoria cast a

glance from him to Chelsea as she glided toward them.

"I can't stay." He pivoted toward their mother and kissed her cheek. "But I'll see you this evening. Say goodbye, Chelsea," he teased back.

"Bye, Ich," she returned, using the nickname she'd given him when they were kids, and laughed as she heard his departing groan.

"Don't let what he said upset you," her mother insisted, indicating she'd overheard.

As much as her brother attempted to discourage her from her business, her mother had always exhibited genuine enthusiasm about it. "I won't," Chelsea said honestly.

"He means well. He's all excited about the little gathering we're having."

Little meant less than two hundred people. "Yes, he is."

Victoria released a soft sigh. "This is what he's always wanted. A life in politics."

Unlike her, he'd been focused for most of his life. "He'll make a good senator."

"Yes, he's quite honest. I do hope he stays that way." She bent forward for a cup and saucer. "Sit now. Have tea with me."

Chelsea joined her at the patio table as she poured the tea.

"Your aunt finally made contact."

With her aunt's scattered manner, that she remembered to do even that was a miracle.

"She sent me a postcard from Senegal." Her mother moved from the chair to pick up Max. "She wrote that she'll be back shortly. I knew you'd want to know," she said, nuzzling his neck. "I also—" Her mother's sudden silence made her look up. "Actually..." She stretched the word. "I wanted to be sure—"

"I was okay?" Chelsea guessed.

"Yes," she said, sounding more at ease. "You never said, but I'm sure this whole situation, having to see Dylan again, has been difficult for you."

"Not too bad," she lied. Chelsea reiterated Dylan's reaction to the news of possible fatherhood and about the DNA test.

"Did you tell him your feelings regarding Maximillian?"

"Yes, I was honest."

Her mother settled Max on her lap. "What was his response?"

Worry skittered through Chelsea, because the question forced her to face reality. She truly didn't know how he felt. He'd never really responded to her adoption announcement.

"Is he going to let you have him?"

Chelsea shrugged away concern for the moment. "Why wouldn't he?"

"Some men view their children as an extension of themselves."

Chelsea believed that was true of her own father in regard to Richman.

"Do you believe he'll let him go?"

"He has his life planned. I don't think he has room in his life to raise a child." To lose Max would rip her apart. She clung to the hope that Dylan didn't believe he was qualified to raise a child. And her aunt had flitted through motherhood once already, leaving Lauren with her mother or a nanny most of the time. "I have to believe that, Mother. I have to."

Chapter Six

Since awakening, Dylan had exercised at the rowing machine, watched an Atlanta Braves game on the sports channel and skimmed the company's bid for a new subdivision. He'd reheated leftovers from last night's dinner out—spaghetti. He'd tried any distraction, but a desire to see Chelsea still existed.

Two years ago he'd dodged his feelings for her. Now fate had thrown a curve and drawn them together again. This time he couldn't stop thinking about her. Yesterday, one thing about her had seemed clear. For a sweet woman, she was tough. Tougher than he'd imagined. Maybe tough enough for him to be honest with her about his feelings.

An affair would provide closure on what existed between them. That was all he would offer. If he made that clear to her, if he was fair to her, then the decision would fall into her lap. But would she even want that with him? She didn't trust him, but she'd kissed him in a way that conveyed they still had unfinished business.

Showered and dressed, he headed for his car. It was dumb to think so much about her. What he'd been contemplating bordered on stupidity. A woman like her didn't have affairs.

With plans to see a movie, a medical thriller that was guaranteed to make him think of something other than her, he drove toward the theater.

Minutes later, he impatiently tapped his fingertips on the steering wheel. In his rearview mirror, he saw cars backed up for nearly a block. The slow-moving train in front of him chugged to a stop and reversed its direction.

Without looking, he fumbled for a CD, hoping for a distraction from his own thoughts. A song about a love lost and found again filled the car. What he felt had nothing to do with love. Others might find it, but not him. How could he? He didn't believe in it.

But Chelsea had probably dreamed about love with some button-down, straitlaced lawyer or investment broker who was looking for a woman to make a home with him, have his children, return his vows of a forever commitment.

That wasn't him, would never be him. As a kid, he'd never fit well in a family. Nothing had changed. He considered himself a loner. His childhood had never included bonding with anyone. Short-term stays at foster homes had taught him that it was best to need no one.

Sure he had friends and a normal social life. In fact, he treasured friendships because he'd been so selective in making them. But family tied a person too tightly to it. And love? What was it really? He'd never known. Sex and friendships carried clearer guidelines. He could deal with them.

Frowning, he looked down and jerked his hand off his cellular phone. He wasn't going to call her. He was simply wondering about Max. The baby was the reason he felt so dissatisfied this morning. That's why he'd nearly picked up the phone to call Chelsea. After all, Max might be his responsibility. His gut constricted with the thought. Though Max was a charmer, he wasn't quite sure he was ready, would ever be ready to be a father.

At the blare of a horn behind him, he noted the green light and hit the gas pedal. Reaching the corner, he turned in the opposite direction of the movie theater.

Sunshine streamed through the windows at the back of Chelsea's house. When she'd padded through the rooms earlier that morning, she'd opened windows, letting the scent of flowers and the morning dampness of yesterday's spring rain seep in.

Unlike the weather, which had improved, her mood had worsened. All night she'd still fretted about what she'd said to Dylan.

Before she'd wandered into the kitchen, she'd decided to stop analyzing everything he'd said, she'd said, or what might happen between them. She had a day of cooking ahead of her for the VanHorns' party.

Because music relaxed her and always made any task more fun, she switched on the stereo and let the country music of the latest female newcomer fill the kitchen with her mellow sound.

To her satisfaction, she managed to get three hours of cooking in and two loads of laundry done before Max awakened. As if he sensed her harried mood, he resisted breakfast. "Come on, honey," she urged when he bubbled another spoonful of oatmeal back at her.

She tried three more spoonfuls, then gave up. Raising a napkin in front of her face, she hid behind it. "Peek-a-boo." As she peered around the edge of it, he giggled, encouraging more play. No matter what she felt, what worry lingered, he brightened her mood.

Sidetracked by her game with him, she was still sitting before him twenty minutes later when the phone rang.

Chelsea set him in his playpen before picking up the receiver.

"You should have taken this job," Tess said as a greeting. "House-sitting at the Farnsworths is like taking a vacation."

"That's not what I want to hear." In the background, a dog yapped. "Tell me you've gotten some of the cooking done."

"I'm basking in sunlight at poolside while the meatballs simmer."

Lounging back in her chair, Chelsea propped her feet on an adjacent one and eyed the washed but unfolded clothes in the laundry basket. "Did you do the fruit flan yet?"

"I'll do it when I get home, then I'll bring the meatballs to your place. By the way, the miniature tarts are done."

With a sigh, Chelsea got up and moved to the stove, beginning to sauté shallots and herbs in a hot skillet. "When did you make the tarts?"

"Midnight. Now that you've checked up on me," she said with amusement, "did you get the phone call from the nominating committee?"

"Yes. They called later that evening." The thrill of her and Tess possibly winning the award hadn't faded.

"Is anything else interesting happening in your life?"

Chelsea wondered if Tess had written a checklist of questions. "Everything is the same."

"The same means Dylan is still around?"

"No." At least not at the moment. The ring of the doorbell saved her from answering more questions. "I have to go."

"We'll talk later," Tess said, indicating she'd only begun her interrogation.

Chelsea set the phone back in its cradle and snatched a quick swallow of the lukewarm tea in her cup. She'd been expecting a delivery from a nearby seafood market.

Before she reached the door, her brother walked in. She always wondered what he would do if he found her in a compromising position with someone. The outlandish thought widened the smile she turned on him. "Hi, Rich." Since she'd seen him yesterday, she discerned he'd come with a purpose.

Looking as if he'd just stepped off the tennis court, he sniffed at the air. "Why all the cooking?" he asked, with a sweep of his arm toward the stove.

"A catering job." Chelsea glanced at the calendar on the wall, pondering her busy schedule. As soon as she finished with the crab cakes, she'd make the call to the market about the delivery that hadn't arrived yet. "The VanHorns' party."

He released what sounded like a pained breath, but said nothing about her business. Bending over the playpen, to Max's delight, he spun one of the circus acrobats on the mobile in the playpen. Cooing, Max kicked at it. "You didn't say if you would help with my campaign."

Chelsea kept an eye on the mixture sizzling in the skillet. All her life, it seemed that what Richman had wanted had always come first with their father. She removed the skillet from the heat.

"That smells wonderful," he said, sidling close. "You're really a good cook, aren't you."

He made her smile. "You don't have to compliment me." She would never turn down her brother.

Amusement glinted in his eyes. "I didn't say that to persuade you." He draped an arm around her shoulder. "Give me a taste."

She lifted the spoon in her hand to his lips. "You always snuck food from the cook, too."

"I was weak to her black Irish pie," he admitted.

"Don't tell anyone you have a weakness," she said in a conspiratorial whisper.

"Never. It's bad for the image." He matched her smile. "So you'll help? You'll be at the gathering?"

"You know I will," she answered easily.

She walked him to the door, even promising to play hostess for an afternoon tea. She'd always been agreeable with him. Always would be—willingly, because she loved him.

In his playpen, Max had flipped to his stomach and was rocking on his knees to move forward. Chelsea laughed. "Pretty soon you'll be all over this house."

Responding to the final rumbling of the washing machine, she hurried into the garage, transferred the last load of clothes to the dryer, then returned to the kitchen to make that call to the market about her delivery. Before she had a chance to pick up the phone, the doorbell rang.

Instead of the teenager from the market, Dylan stood before her. She took in his wind-tossed hair, his worn jeans and faded T-shirt and felt pleasure at seeing him again, but she had so much to do today. She didn't have time for any distractions.

"Can I come in?" He noted that she didn't look annoyed—or pleased to see him. "I came to offer you a deal." He passed her in the doorway. "Hi, Max."

Chelsea stared after him. He was already in the kitchen, lifting Max into his arms. A different wave of emotion swept over her. "What deal?" she asked, anxious at the way he was giving Max his full attention.

"You're sticky," Dylan said with a laugh, wiping a finger gently at Max's cheek.

"Applesauce." Chelsea narrowed the distance between them. "What deal?" she repeated, puzzled. She'd expected him to keep his distance.

Holding Max, he circled the kitchen while gauging how to approach her with an idea. "I always liked this house."

Chelsea cast an impatient look at him. She had liked it, too. Unlike the huge house she'd grown up in, the bungalow had flaws—a water heater that rattled, a window that stuck in summer. Not perfect, but it suited her.

Jeans and a baggy blue sweatshirt made her look like a teenager. Temptation slithered through him to slip his hands beneath the sweatshirt, feel her slimness. "Why didn't you ever use that room?" he asked, gesturing toward it.

The room addition had been a painful reminder to her of what had happened before between them. Initially, she'd planned to use it as an office. But she'd left for Europe, spent more than a year there, and when she'd returned months ago, she'd been too busy to bother with decorating. "My life-style changed. I was out of the country for a while. When I came back, it was because my father had died, then Tess and I launched Chores Galore."

Dylan prepared for her refusal even as he spoke. "Since I'll be around—because of Max, I have to do something while I'm here. I'll paint the room for you."

Seizing a quick breath, Chelsea felt a flicker of fear. He wanted to be around Max. Did he plan to take him from her? If he had the parental right, she wouldn't have a legal stand to stop him.

Dylan noted her sudden paleness. "Look," he quickly added, "I'm not sure what I'm going to do.

But if he's mine, I can't be a stranger to him.'' Her silence wasn't helping him. "What do you say? Are you going to let me finish what I started?"

Let me finish what I started. Was he talking about the room or them? How foolish she still was. He preferred glossy, one-dimensional women who asked nothing of him. That would never be her. She analyzed everything, thought and acted with her heart. "The day after tomorrow is fine with me, if that's when you want to paint."

Dylan smiled at her bare feet and the hot pink nail polish on her toenails. "That works for me."

"Fine." Pivoting away in response to the doorbell, she released an unsteady sigh. What was happening here?

While she dealt with the delivery from Wharfside Seafood Market, Dylan amused Max. Actually, the baby entertained him with his gibberish. His eyes wide with curiosity, he sought the movement in the other room. Dylan, too, cast a look to see Chelsea stuffing bags of food in the refrigerator. "All of that is for the party?"

She nodded, then exchanged a check with the delivery boy for the last bag of seafood.

Patting Max's back, Dylan ambled toward her. She shoved a bag of shrimp on a refrigerator shelf. She would be busy today; she didn't need him around. "Will you make enough to counter your expenses?" he questioned while lowering Max into his playpen.

His business tone stirred her smile. "Yes, we figured that out."

He'd have expected her to have a good mind for business. She was logical, sensible.

"I went into this business with Tess with a clear head." She set a bag of crab legs on the table. "We knew we could make the business work for two years with our investment, but we needed to start making a profit by then."

Knowing her background, Dylan asked the obvious question. "Your family would help, wouldn't they?"

She reared back as if he'd said the unspeakable. "I never asked them for money. I had to do this on my own."

Dylan straddled a kitchen chair to watch her. On first impression, she appeared to be an unassuming, quiet person. He'd even heard someone, a woman at Richman's birthday celebration, describe her as a brown wren. How wrong people were. The Chelsea he knew had guts and tenacity. Beneath the slim, delicate appearance, she hid a woman with resilience and unstoppable spirit. "I saw your brother."

Chelsea wondered if Richman had played politician or drilled him with questions about Max. "What did he say?"

"Hi." Dylan cracked a grin. It faded instantly as he noted the slight frown etching a line between her brows. "He said that he came to get your help with his campaign. Do you think he has aspirations to live in the White House?"

Memories crowded her. "I don't know if he does, but that was our father's plan for him."

He viewed the pile of crab legs she was tackling with a cracker. "What are you making?"

"Crabmeat patties." She abandoned the crab legs to roll potatoes out of their sack and onto the counter. If she didn't do more than one project at a time, she would never finish everything.

"And you?" Dylan questioned. "What did your father want you to do?"

"I never measured up to the Huntsford image, especially with my father." As a child, she'd always been afraid of doing the wrong thing. As an adult, she'd faced her flaw. She hadn't been timid or shy, just fearful of doing something that would rouse her father's disapproval. Not once before her father had died had he told her he was proud of her, or that he loved her. "Richman came first with our father."

Unknowingly, he'd touched a raw spot, Dylan discerned. Though he had no idea what she planned to do with the potatoes, he grabbed a potato peeler.

Chelsea gave him a second look. "You know how to peel potatoes?"

More than one foster home had believed children worked for their keep. "I have hidden talents."

She didn't want to know about them. She really didn't.

Idly, Dylan's gaze roamed over her face. As always she'd pulled her hair back, but wispy tendrils framed her cheeks. "What are you going to make with the potatoes?"

"Potato nests. They're shredded potatoes shaped like birds' nests." Her blood growing warmer beneath his intense stare, she hurriedly pulled out the shredder from a bottom cupboard.

Dylan dropped a potato in the pot of water she'd set near him. "So your brother was the favored one."

"Always." Chelsea dumped the herbs and measured bread crumbs into the bowl with the crabmeat.

Dylan hadn't deciphered any jealousy in her voice. She'd made the previous comments matter-of-factly. In fact, he heard more affection than resentment in her voice when she discussed her brother.

Chelsea cracked eggs into a bowl. "Richman had more ambition than me." She stirred the mixture. "My lack of direction bothered my father the most." She formed a patty and set it in the skillet.

"Some people take longer to find their way."

Kind. That was the kindest thing he'd ever said to her.

"What about your mother?" He recalled Victoria Huntsford as a smiling woman with a soft voice and a sweetness she'd obviously passed on to her daughter. "What did she say?"

"She accepted everything I ever did," she said over the sound of more crab cakes sautéing. "But most of the time, I was out of step with what was expected of me." She'd tried her hand at so many things, searching for success—to please her father. But she'd always felt so inadequate, incompetent around him.

Dylan truly didn't understand her need for approval by her father. There had never been anyone he was that close to, cared about that much. But he understood rejection. The most damaging came from someone you loved. He knew; he'd been there. "You're successful at what you do. Don't you think your father would approve now?''

That was easy to answer. She released a mirthless laugh. ''Never. And I know my brother's worried. That I've decided to include cleaning houses in my business isn't exactly the type of achievement he'd hoped for.''

The potato peeler in his hand, he slowly looked up. Wonderful aromas filled the kitchen. On a desk in her living room, two hundred and fifty wedding invitations were addressed and stamped. A calendar on the wall listed jobs-to-do written in red, follow-up jobs in blue, jobs that might be referrals in yellow. ''That makes no sense. You're an efficiency expert.''

She blushed at the unexpected tribute.

''Did that compliment make you nervous?''

''You make me nervous,'' she blurted out, taking a step from the stove to wash her hands of the fishy smell.

After so much time thinking about her, he felt some satisfaction in knowing she wasn't as ambivalent as she tried to convey. ''Why?''

She blew out a breath. She wasn't pretty enough, funny enough, sexy enough. ''Because I'm not your type,'' she said with conviction over the sound of rushing water. ''So I know if you say something nice like that, then you must mean it.''

A grin sprang to his face. ''Lousy of me.''

''Dylan, I'm serious.'' And confused. *Again.* Why had he kissed her yesterday?

''You're always too serious,'' he said, bridging the space between them. In the sunlight in the room, red highlights shone in her hair. Tempted, he toyed with a soft, sweet-smelling strand near her ear, curling it around his finger.

"Here I am," a breezy feminine voice announced behind them.

Chelsea jerked back.

Dylan rounded a scowl on the intruder. Just as quickly, he silently thanked the woman. Though initially annoyed at her friend's interruption, he viewed her timing as perfect. Another moment and all the willpower he prided himself in having would have fled. Chelsea would have been in his arms, her taste a part of him again.

Gaping, Tess stood frozen. Because of their close friendship, she'd walked in. Why wouldn't she? She hadn't expected anyone there but Chelsea. With what appeared to be an effort, she dragged her gaze from Dylan to Chelsea.

Chelsea managed the expected introduction. "This is Tess."

Nervous with Tess's meaningful gaze fixed on her, Chelsea skirted the table to alleviate her friend of the dish filled with meatballs. "I started the crab cakes." She scurried away with the dish. "The lobster medallions are done," she rambled, "and I marinated the salmon rosettes overnight."

Tess sidled close to her at the counter and snagged her hands to stop their fluttering.

Chelsea's shoulders drooped. She needed to get a grip. Across the room, Dylan scooped up Max as if he'd been doing it since the day Max was born, then wandered with him into Max's bedroom.

"I'll take the rosettes home and caramelize the onions," Tess said in a louder tone than necessary for Dylan's benefit. "What was going on?" she suddenly whispered when Dylan disappeared.

"I don't know," Chelsea said honestly.

"I saw the way he was looking at you."

Chelsea lifted the cover from the casserole. Tess's observation made what she'd felt real and not some fantasy of her mind. "These smell heavenly."

"Chel, is he different now?"

Yes, he kissed me this time. The little voice in her head nagged again. Don't forget that he walked away without a look back last time. If he did it once, he could do that to her again. He wouldn't even be in her life now if it weren't for Max. She needed to keep her feet firmly planted, not let a few compliments and tender touches make her play the fool. Experienced, he might be lulling her for his own purpose. Perhaps he was beginning to really want Max. "Tell me if the rosettes look okay."

Tess snagged her arm before she could open the refrigerator. "Chel, you're not going to distract me."

"No one could," Chelsea teased. Her friend possessed unbelievable persistence. One time she'd staked out the house of a client with an unpaid bill.

"Have you slept with him?" Tess asked quietly.

Chelsea avoided her friend's inquiring stare and glanced toward Max's bedroom. What was Dylan doing in there? "I can't believe you asked that."

"Don't be angry with me. I don't want to see you hurt."

Chelsea touched her shoulder, then reached into the refrigerator. "I'm not angry."

"It might be good if you did get angry now and then. Now, preferably. Most women would be angry at him for breaking off with her to start seeing someone else, especially if it's someone she knows."

"Would that change anything?" Chelsea set the casserole dish containing the salmon rosettes in her arms.

Tess shook her head in resignation. "Honey, remember you need some nice man who's ready to settle down."

"I'll remember." Chelsea ushered her to the door.

When they reached it, Tess balked from moving. "Did you look for a new dress yet?"

Chelsea hadn't told her that she probably wouldn't be going to the award dinner—it was the same night as Richman's gathering. "Not yet."

"We'll have to go shopping together," Tess said, with the same enthusiasm she'd displayed when they'd learned of their nomination.

There was no point in putting off the inevitable, Chelsea decided. "I may not go."

"What!" Tess's voice rose an octave. "How can you not go? Entrepreneur of the Year in a Small Business," she announced, measuring each word as if Chelsea hadn't heard them before. "You're a nominee. No," she said adamantly. "*You* are Chores Galore. You thought of the idea. You drum up business. You do the scheduling. I can't go alone. Chel, you have to go with me."

With Dylan in the next room, Chelsea didn't want to argue the point. "We'll talk later."

Tess muttered something unintelligible before offering a parting comment that she would pick up the refrigerated truck for tomorrow's party.

Chelsea closed the door but didn't shut out the advice her friend had offered. Whatever was happening with Dylan was temporary.

She hoped one day to find a man who would love her, who would want marriage and children and commitment. But that man might never come her way. After her twenty-eighth birthday, she'd begun to resign herself to not having that fantasy come true, as one by one friends of hers had gotten engaged, as she'd taken the role of bridesmaid too many times and had watched them marry, then had played hostess for baby showers. But even if she found that man, would he do the one thing Dylan did do to her? Would he thrill her?

Curiosity piqued at the quietness from Max's bedroom, she wandered toward it. Ever since Tess's arrival, Dylan had been in there. Had he disappeared to give her privacy with a friend? At the bedroom doorway, Chelsea stopped.

On the changing table, Max thrashed at the air while Dylan undid his diaper.

"After I change this, you go to sleep. I've sung my share of songs," he said softly, and slid a diaper under Max's small bottom. Max's large dark eyes remained riveted on him. "If you're mine—" Dylan ran his large hand lovingly over Max's soft, downy hair. "If you're mine, don't worry. I'll be here for you."

Chelsea's heart softened. She tried to steel herself to her own weakness. He'd already proved he could hurt her, but no man could touch a baby so gently and not possess a wealth of love.

Chapter Seven

Before he saw her, Chelsea retreated to the kitchen. She couldn't allow the tenderness she'd witnessed to touch her too deeply. Why wouldn't Dylan be that way with Max? He was sweet, attentive, responsive. Anyone would be. Or would they? she countered. She couldn't recall ever seeing Alan touch Max that way, talk to him so gently.

"Max is awake but making noises at that mobile," Dylan suddenly said from behind her.

"I bought that for him right after he was born." Uneasy from her own thoughts, she focused on slicing a lemon. "He favors the bear, though he talks to the donkey, too."

Dylan inched closer to see what she was making. On the counter, she'd left a sheet with a long list of jobs to do from washing parsley to rolling brioche dough. "He doesn't talk."

Clearly they both were avoiding discussion about what had happened before between them. "Yes, he does."

A smile flitted through Dylan's words. "He babbles."

She finished the lemon twists and made a few green onion flowers to use as garnishes. She mused that he couldn't really believe Max couldn't "talk," or he wouldn't have stood there chatting to him as if he'd understood every word.

Dylan scanned the disorder in her kitchen. He needed to leave her alone or level with her about what he wanted from her. But what he could give her was suddenly clear. "Who's going to watch Max while you're working tomorrow?"

That was one problem she hadn't completely solved yet.

"Mrs. Baines," she said, referring to their employee, though the woman would have to take Max with her to a doctor's appointment.

Dylan couldn't stop himself. Later, he'd analyze why. "I could watch him."

Chelsea tugged at her bottom lip. What was his plan?

"Why?" she asked warily.

Unknowingly, she delivered tough questions. He saw distrust in the darkening of her eyes. He shrugged. "I don't know." Hell, that wasn't true. "Being around him feels right," he admitted with some surprise at his own words.

Chelsea scowled with more annoyance, not at him but herself. But trusting him again was a giant step. "If you really want to."

"Said so, didn't I? So what time tomorrow?"

Her stomach tensed. She hadn't expected him to be so comfortable with Max. "I don't understand. You don't even think he's your son."

"What if I am?" There it was. The big question. He couldn't get that one out of his head. To go on with his life as if nothing was happening would be impossible. No child should be ignored by its parent. The possibility that he was Max's father weighed too heavily on him to walk away as if Max didn't exist. Until he had an answer, he felt a need to be around him.

Chelsea shrugged. Was he really beginning to care about Max? "Eleven."

"By the way—" Dylan paused at the door, a hand braced against the door frame "—congratulations."

Watching the door close behind him, Chelsea grimaced. How much more of what Tess had said, like the question about them sleeping together, had he overheard?

By ten the next morning and another early wake up, she had only to dab the finishing touches, spoonfuls of whipped cream, on top of fruit tarts.

With Max teething and crankier than usual, she pulled out the sling support that nestled him close to her breast and hauled him around with her while she soaked dirty dishes and packed ones for serving.

Within a few minutes, he snoozed, giving her time to shower and dress.

She hoped she would stop feeling like the heroine in the *Perils of Pauline*. First, Dylan changed her flat tire, then because of her episode with the flu, she had to call him to take Max. Now she was imposing on him for another baby-sitting job. She even had him playing painter for her.

When she first came to his apartment, she hardly expected to instigate this much contact. Chelsea stilled in zipping her dress. Wait a minute. Except for the flu, she hadn't done anything. Dylan had been coming to her home, initiating everything, volunteering.

In the kitchen again, she sipped a cup of tea. Why? Oh, she didn't need this, didn't have time to analyze everything he did. She was already dealing with her fair share of nerves because of the party.

With the ring of the doorbell, she nearly dropped the cup. "Just a minute," she called out. Relax. She repeated the word like a mantra, then opened the door.

Dylan walked in to the sound of country music and her looking like springtime in a dress with small pink-and-purple flowers that loosely followed her curves and flowed over her hips to her ankles. Her hair was pulled back, emphasizing the lighter strands above her ears, which were adorned with small pearl earrings.

"I'm glad you got here early." Head bent, she slipped on her low-heeled pumps.

Dylan glanced at Max stirring in his playpen.

"What do you need carried down? I'll do it while you finish up."

Chelsea pointed behind her to the kitchen counter. "The microwave. Tess is bringing hers, too." On edge, she fiddled with a pin in her hair. "We assume with two of them, plus the one at the VanHorns', and the oven, we'll be able to heat everything."

Hearing the nervous edge in her voice, Dylan paused beside her and brushed a knuckle across her cheek. "You'll do fine."

"Cool as a cucumber. See?" she said with a strained laugh, holding out steady hands.

Dylan returned a smile because she seemed to need it. What he wanted was to crush her to him. He wanted to kiss her again. He was craving the feel of her lips against his. He just hadn't known how badly he desired that until this moment.

With those gray eyes on her, a fluttery sensation coursed through her. When he turned away, she ran damp hands down the skirt of her dress. Instead of calming her, without doing anything except being there, he'd tensed her more. She sighed with disgust. No, he hadn't. She was doing it to herself, letting her imagination make too much of nothing.

"Tess is here," Dylan announced, reentering the house. "I'll take Max in the van, drive this stuff there and come back later with the van. Tess thought it was a good idea."

Double-crossed by her most loyal and trusted friend. Since Tess had had reservations about Dylan yesterday, what had happened to cause her turnabout regarding him? During the drive with her in the refrigerated truck, Chelsea pinned her down for an answer.

"He made sense." Tess rolled her eyes at her own weakness to him. "He was persuasive. Everything he said sounded as if all he cared about was your welfare."

Chelsea shifted her attention from the two-lane highway. "Such as?"

"He said he would take care of Max so you wouldn't have to worry about him, and he would cart in our equipment so we weren't worn out before we began."

In the rearview mirror, Chelsea stared at Dylan driving her van. Why? Why such helpfulness from a man who had wanted nothing to do with her two years ago? Why was he acting so differently now? She frowned at the rarely felt cynicism. She usually accepted people at face value and didn't look for ulterior motives.

But deep down, she didn't believe in him. No, she didn't believe in the possibility of him and her. So every time he did anything kind or he touched her, and especially when he kissed her, she couldn't help wondering why.

By the time guests began to arrive that evening, she and Tess had set up small tables beneath the white canopies on the terrace and the lawn of the VanHorns' estate. Small bouquets of flowers added color. Crystal gleamed beneath the white Italian lights, and ladened with the long buffet table was serving dishes.

Chelsea plastered a smile on her face and stood with Tess behind the serving table to help guests.

Across the manicured lawn, her mother wiggled her fingers in a wave.

"Who's the man with her?" Tess mumbled out of the corner of her mouth.

"My mother describes him as 'a gentleman caller,'" Chelsea said, referring to the tall man with the full head of white hair.

Tess raised her brows.

Chelsea restrained a giggle and dished out a second helping of her chicken to a rotund man with a Texas drawl.

"He loves your food," Tess teased after he'd walked away.

With satisfaction, Chelsea noticed the guests had made a hearty dent in all of the dishes.

"I think we did it," Tess said in a joyful whisper when all the guests were seated and eating.

Chelsea nodded agreeably. A sense of achievement filling her with pride abated all trace of nervousness. Along with Tess, she made repeated trips carrying dishes back to the kitchen. For the next hour, she had her hands plunged in dishwater.

"I'm pooped," Tess muttered while packing up the washed serving dishes. "But it was fun."

From the kitchen's french windows, Chelsea watched departing guests. One of them glided in her direction.

Wearing a soft aqua dress with chiffon sleeves, her mother breezed in and planted a kiss on Chelsea's cheek. "You did a marvelous job." She swept a smile from Chelsea to Tess. "Your food, ladies, was the hit of the party."

Chelsea exchanged a pleased smile with Tess.

"I have a marvelous idea." Her mother's face brightened. "Why don't you cater Richman's party two weeks from this Friday?"

Peripherally, Chelsea caught Tess's frown.

"Mrs. Huntsford, we couldn't. That's the night of the—"

Chelsea cut in before Tess mentioned the award dinner. "It's too big of a job for us, Mother. We aren't prepared for that."

"Really?" She frowned, obviously puzzled because the VanHorn party hadn't been small. "Well you know best. But if you change your mind, let me know by next weekend." As if something more weighty had entered her mind, her frown deepened, and her eyes darted around the room. "Where is Max? Who's watching him?"

Tess's scowl lessened. Chelsea expected her friend to drill her later, now that she knew the reason why Chelsea had said she wouldn't attend the award dinner. At the moment, though, Tess was preoccupied, piping in too helpfully, "Dylan."

Chelsea didn't miss the quick arch of her mother's brow. "Dylan? He's getting involved in your life again?"

"In Max's, Mother."

"I see."

Chelsea had never heard two words imply so much before. "We're on a friendly basis because of—" She grew silent as her mother looked past her.

She beamed, polite pleasure entering her voice. "Dylan, how nice to see you again."

Chelsea traced her stare to Dylan standing at the doorway. Holding Max in his carrier seat, Dylan flashed a smile few women could resist. "How are you, Mrs. Huntsford?"

"Victoria, please," she insisted, and ambled over to look at Max. "He's so adorable, isn't he?"

Dylan said nothing. He didn't have to. His eyes softened as he looked tenderly at Max. And Max was bonding, too. He'd curled his tiny hand around one of Dylan's fingers while he gurgled a few sounds at him. *Whatever happens, one of us will be hurt at having to let Max go,* Chelsea now knew.

"Watch Max," Dylan said, "and I'll carry everything to your van for you."

Chelsea snapped herself from her thoughts to find everyone staring at her. She didn't miss the look of speculation in her mother's eyes.

"How interesting," her mother murmured the moment the door closed behind Dylan.

To avoid more discussion, Chelsea took on a matter-of-fact tone. "He's been helpful."

Looking like part of some silent conspiracy, Tess and her mother merely grinned at each other.

They could imagine and interpret his helping any way they wanted. Chelsea made a quick escape out the door.

"I'll take the refrigerated truck back," Tess said, suddenly behind her.

Any protest Chelsea planned remained silent. Tess scurried to the truck, leaving her to drive home with

Dylan. Sighing at what seemed like unexpected matchmaking, Chelsea returned to the house for Max.

Exhaustion seeping over her minutes later when she was sitting beside Dylan, she rested her head on the back of the seat and closed her eyes.

"Tired?"

"Wonderfully."

"It was a lot of hard work."

She raised a hand and blocked a yawn. "I don't mind hard work."

Nearing an intersection, Dylan kept his eyes on traffic. She didn't need to tell him that. She'd worked every moment he was with her the day before and probably for hours after he'd left.

"Was Max okay today?"

With a look her way, he saw her lips were curved in a satisfied smile. "We went to the zoo."

Chelsea angled a look at him. "You did?" She would never have envisioned him pushing a stroller along zoo paths.

Dylan negotiated a turn. "He's a little young. He got kind of wide-eyed when we stopped by the elephants. And he wailed at the monkeys."

"I'll have to take him again when he's older." *If I still have him.* As quickly as the depressing thought formed, she pushed it away. "That's the first time he's ever gone there."

"Me, too."

She shifted on the seat toward him. "You've never been to a zoo before?"

"One of those experiences lacking from my childhood," he said in an offhand manner that Chelsea didn't believe.

"Your family never—"

"I have no family," he said emotionlessly.

The thought of no family clenched her heart. She might not have always pleased hers, but she'd always felt as if she belonged. "I know you feel that way about your father, but what about your mother?"

Old memories, some he wanted to forget, lingered close to the surface. "I spent my share of time in foster homes."

The edge to his voice spoke volumes. Not all of the experiences had been pleasant. "Dylan, I'm so sorry."

"Why? You didn't know me. You weren't responsible."

But her heart ached for the sadness he must have endured as a child.

"My mother got pregnant and wasn't pleased about it. It would slow her down, end her fun."

She couldn't imagine a mother abandoning her child. Anger so rarely felt rose within her. "Who told you that?" she asked, wondering if as a child he'd gathered facts incorrectly.

"My grandmother." He braked for a red light. "I lived with her until I was seven."

"Where was your mother?"

"She'd taken off with some man. My grandmother never said too much about her, until one day." Dylan tightened his fingers on the steering wheel and felt impatience rise for the light to change. "I was five.

She told me my mother was dead. It meant nothing to me. I didn't know her, had never known her."

Instinctively Chelsea leaned closer to see him better in the dark confines of the car. "You said you were seven when you went to a foster home?"

"Almost eight." With the change of the light, he hit the accelerator harder than necessary. There was more, too much more that he never wanted to remember. "I'd had a birthday two days after I went there."

Had anyone remembered it, thought about it? Her heart twisted for the child he'd been, who'd had no mother and then lost his grandmother, and had been forgotten in the system. She wanted to move near, touch his hand and make contact with him, make up for all the people who'd passed through his life and hadn't cared. In that instant, with him sharing so much, she didn't feel so sensible, didn't feel anything except the emotions coursing through her for him.

Dylan stiffened his spine against the mood slipping over him. The hurt belonged to the child he'd been, not the man he was. He'd vowed never to let it control him again. Glancing her way, he saw too much sympathy in her eyes.

"Dylan—" A sensitive soul, a compassionate one, she'd always opened her heart too wide to others. The pressure behind her lids growing heavier, with an aching heart, she thought about Max. She vowed he would never know such misery.

"Forget it," he snapped.

Chelsea froze from his curtness. Perhaps reaching out to him had been a mistake. What made her think he'd want any emotional closeness with her?

Play **TIC-TAC-TOE** and get **FREE GIFTS**

HOW TO PLAY:

1. Play the tic-tac-toe scratch-off game at the right for your FREE BOOKS and FREE GIFT!

2. Send back this card and you'll receive TWO brand-new Silhouette Special Edition® novels. These books have a cover price of $4.25 each, but they are yours to keep absolutely free.

3. There's no catch. You're under no obligation to buy anything. We charge nothing — ZERO — for your first shipment. And you don't have to make any minimum number of purchases — not even one!

4. The fact is, thousands of readers enjoy receiving books by mail from the Silhouette Reader Service™ months before they're available in stores. They like the convenience of home delivery, and they love our discount prices!

5. We hope that after receiving your free books you'll want to remain a subscriber. But the choice is yours — to continue or cancel, any time at all! So why not take us up on our invitation, with no risk of any kind. You'll be glad you did!

YOURS **FREE**
A FABULOUS **MYSTERY GIFT!**

**We can't tell you what it is...
but we're sure you'll like it!**
A FREE GIFT —
just for playing
TIC-TAC-TOE!

DETACH AND MAIL CARD TODAY!

First, scratch the gold boxes on the tic-tac-toe board. Then remove the "X" sticker from the front and affix it so that you get three X's in a row. This means you can get TWO FREE Silhouette Special Edition® novels and a **FREE MYSTERY GIFT!**

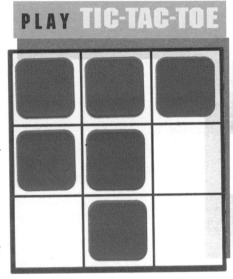

PLAY TIC-TAC-TOE

YES! Please send me all the gifts for which I qualify. I understand that I am under no obligation to purchase any books, as explained on the back of this card.

(U-SIL-SE-08/98)

235 SDL CH6U

Name		
	(PLEASE PRINT CLEARLY)	
Address		Apt.#
City	State	Zip

Dylan grimaced as she averted her face and stared out the window. He'd shot his mouth off. All she'd done was offer understanding. Youthful resentment never completely vanished, but it had nothing to do with her. She hadn't deserved the anger that had been meant for another woman. "I'm sorry."

Her eyes turned on him, filled with honest openness. "You didn't have to say that."

He made the final turn down her street. She was giving him the easy way out. He owed her more. "Yes, I did."

Chelsea delivered a strained smile, but she ached for him. Had he ever had a birthday party, gone to an amusement park, had friends over to play? She thought of the loneliness he must have endured. He'd suffered. Everyone needed someone. Deep down, he had to know that. But after years of guarding himself from more disappointment and pain, had he convinced himself differently?

Dylan wondered when his tongue had developed such looseness. Annoyed with himself, he zipped the van into the driveway. "I'll carry everything in for you," he offered, to distract her. Mostly he would keep his mouth shut.

Uncertain, Chelsea pushed open her door. "You can leave everything. I'll bring it all in tomorrow morning."

Dylan unclicked his seat belt. So she'd decided to keep her distance. That was for the best. He slid out from behind the steering wheel and rounded the back of the van to lift Max from it.

Chelsea was already bending inside to unfasten

him. Before he did anything else he'd regret, he
needed to leave. "Here." He handed the van keys to
her.

Chelsea could have left it at that, but he'd shared
more than she'd expected. All day he'd been there for
her. "I want to thank you for your help today. You
made it a lot easier for me."

"It was nothing." *Don't thank me for anything.
I'm going to hurt you again.* Dylan looked at Max.
His dark eyes were riveted to him. *Don't rely on me.*
Dylan wished he was old enough to understand.

Chelsea sighed at his refusal to accept her gratitude.
"Whether you like it or not, you're a kind man."
Holding Max, she angled her body to shield him as
she leaned closer to Dylan. Before she considered her
actions further, she eased up on her toes and pressed
a kiss to his cheek. "Thank you."

As much as he wanted to, he couldn't pretend he
was only with her because of Max. "I'm not kind,"
he said huskily. "You know that better than anyone
else."

"Then why have you helped me so much?"

Hadn't he always sensed the complexity of this
woman, sensed, too, she could draw him to her unlike
any other woman ever had? A man couldn't touch her
skin and not wonder if it was as soft everywhere.

"You said not to kiss you again. Did you mean
that?"

A faint shock wave shot down her spine like a
warning. She could lie. Of course, she couldn't.
"No." Demanding herself to stay calm, she held her

ground even as his fingers caressed the line of her jaw.

"Good." For too long he'd been thinking about kissing her again. Like a man dying of thirst, he closed his mouth over hers to take his fill. He couldn't be gentle when need sped through him.

With a long, lingering kiss, one so thorough it rocked him, he tried his damnedest to get her out of his system. But he knew this wouldn't be enough. Fantasies tumbled around in his mind. There was passion in her lips, seductiveness in the slender body pressed close to his. No matter how much he tried to rid himself of her, he'd never forgotten what might have been. And the "what if" in their relationship was like an aphrodisiac drawing him to her, making him ache.

The regret Dylan anticipated later slammed at him instantly when he drew back. Her eyes bore a dazed confusion. His hands tightened on delicate, slender arms. Breakable. A reminder of sorts. He couldn't forget her vulnerability, lack of guile, unselfishness or total honesty, which had charmed him from the first moment they'd met.

Through his childhood, he'd dealt with people who'd said one thing and meant another. We'll keep you for as long as we can, they'd tell him. And within a week he'd be sent to another foster home. Honesty belonged in someone else's life, not his.

Then he'd met her. In her shy smile, he'd seen beauty. In those blue eyes, he'd seen trust. In her, he'd found someone more open and honest than anyone he'd ever met. Later he might regret saying too much, but at the moment, he needed to tell her how special he thought she was. "You tempt me."

The soft huskiness in his voice washed over her. She swayed toward him, feeling as if her legs might buckle beneath her. Speaking proved impossible. Moving away never entered her mind.

"Forget I said that," he murmured now.

"I can't." How could she? Beneath her hand at his chest, his heart beat strong and steady. The heat and strength of his body tingled her fingertips.

"You need to," he murmured as her scent filled him.

Kiss me again. She wanted him to. She wanted to find all that she'd ever imagined with him. "Can you?"

Not too steady, he let his fingers trail down her slender jaw. "No," he whispered.

As he turned away, her pulse thudded, her blood pounded. And he had her longing for what she'd denied wanting.

Chapter Eight

More tired than she realized, Chelsea overslept the next morning. Clouds hung low and the heaviness of an incoming rain clung to the air as she hustled Max into the van.

When traffic backed up on the freeway, she switched the radio on to a country music station. The next exit was hers. If she got there in a few minutes, she would arrive on time for Max's check-up at the doctor's office.

They were late, but only by a few minutes. Out of sorts, she appreciated the coolness of the air-conditioning in the pediatrician's office. She liked being punctual. That's all that was wrong.

Liar, her mind screamed. Feelings for Dylan had grown more confusing. She told herself that romanticizing about him amounted to stupidity. He didn't think about her when he wasn't with her the way she did about him. He didn't want to be with her, to hear her voice, to feel the heat churning within him during another kiss. She wanted all that and more.

You have no pride, she berated herself. *This man tossed you aside.* He chose a woman she would never compare to. Well, maybe with plastic surgery and body molding, she might resemble someone like Lauren. But a person was stuck with their personality. She lacked the effervescence, the quick wit and charm that he wanted in a woman. Repeatedly she'd warned herself not to make too much of his kisses. They may have been incited by nothing more than curiosity, or some ego trip on his part to see if he could make her swoon.

Oh, but the man she'd been with yesterday hadn't seemed like that. Helping her, he'd been thoughtful. When talking about his past, he'd been vulnerable. He'd been the man she'd seen glimpses of during their brief time together. "Max, I don't know what I'll do if he's your daddy." If he was, she might never see either of them again.

There. That was what this was all about. Max was a part of her soul already. She'd known that the moment she'd held him.

And Dylan? She wanted him to want her so badly that he would feel as if he was going crazy with his need for her. And even as she wanted to spark emotion in him, she wasn't certain she was prepared for the consequences of such an act.

A downpour began before ten that morning. Locking the trailer door, Dylan saw the last of the crew at the job site driving away. Trudging through the muddy ground, he cursed the weather, expecting to get behind schedule. He stopped beside his car and scraped muck off the bottom of his work boots before sliding in. And he swore again.

Windshield wipers swished. His discontent intensified. In no mood for the solitude of his apartment, he drove to the paint store, then to Chelsea's on the chance he'd see her—because he needed to see her. That bothered him a lot. Since he was nine years old, he'd made sure he never needed anyone. He'd learned then to be satisfied with only his own company. But the desire to see her, to hear her voice, overshadowed thoughts of doing anything else.

His disgruntled mood intensified at not seeing her van in the driveway. He should have called first. She could be picking someone up from the airport, cleaning a house. She could be anywhere for hours. It made no sense to wait around for her.

He wheeled around a corner and zipped into the parking lot of a fast-food restaurant. For the next half hour, he nursed a cup of coffee. When in his car again, he flicked on a CD. The heavy strains of Mozart matched his troubled mood. It bordered on stupidity to ride around in circles like some school kid, waiting for, hoping for the sight of one girl. He would try one more time. No more. He'd never waited for any woman, never had any reason to.

Once more, he drove down her street. Half a block from her house, he saw a police cruiser parked in front of it. Something akin to fear gripped him. In his whole life he'd never felt it for another person. Now two people roused it within him.

Cursing, he screeched his car to a halt in front of her house and jumped out. In the rain, he sprinted to her front door and barreled in. "Chelsea!" As he yelled her name, heads swiveled toward him.

One of two uniformed officers stepped forward.

Dylan brushed past him to reach her. "What happened?" he asked even as his eyes assessingly skimmed her for injury. "Where's Max? Is he all right?"

Seeing what appeared to be panic in his eyes, she reached out and touched his arm. "Dylan, he's okay."

"What the hell happened, then?" he asked, with a glance at the officers.

"Someone broke into my garage." Rain dripped from his dark hair. Glossy from the moisture, the dark strands behind his ears flared out in unruly curls. Raindrops beaded his face, stirring a temptation within her to press her fingertips against the wetness on his lean cheeks. "You're drenched."

"It's raining." Dressed in faded jeans, an oversize sweatshirt and tennis shoes, she looked too young to have such problems. He gave the living room a sweeping look to make sure everything was in order.

"Looks like kids," the one officer commented matter-of-factly, as if it were nothing serious. "They broke into the garage, but not the house. You said a ten-speed is missing?"

Chelsea assumed that to a policeman, because he'd

seen so much worse, her problem was minor. But to her it was devastating. "Yes. And some tools."

"Is that all you had in the garage?"

"My business equipment, too." The stolen items meant nothing. The damage to her supplies made her want to cry.

Dylan's frown deepened at the emotion that cracked her voice. Protective instincts rose within him. He wanted to draw her in his arms, console her.

"Miss." The older officer prevented more discussion. "We'll file a report. Get a new lock."

Her back straightening, she nodded, then saw them to the door.

Because he'd been through rough times, understood the mettle needed to get past them, Dylan admired what he saw emerging in her. It was that spirit, that undeniable spirit, that captivated him. A shallow woman wouldn't reveal the same kind of grit during adversity. "How bad is the damage?" he asked when she returned.

"See for yourself." She led the way into the garage. "Leave the door open," she said, referring to the one that connected the kitchen to the garage. "I want to hear Max if he wakes up."

At the garage doorway, Dylan looked past her. Someone had dumped soaps used for cleaning, cut hoses to a vacuum cleaner and floor polisher, dropped and broken a microwave, and crashed serving dishes she'd used only yesterday to cater the VanHorns' party. "You're insured, aren't you?"

"Yes." But she would have to buy new supplies now or not accept any jobs.

"Where were you earlier?"

Chelsea slipped off her sneakers and socks. "Max had a doctor's appointment."

"He's sick?"

"No." She heard the trace of worry in his voice. "He needed a check-up." Barefoot, she sloshed a mop around the floor to dry up the splattered soap.

Dylan grabbed a stack of Chores Galore advertising flyers soaked from the soap dumped over them and tossed them in the trash bin nearby. "For what?"

Rain softly pattered against the garage roof. Chelsea glanced at the small garage window. Streams of water rolled down it. "Because it was time for an immunization." Despite her recent problem, she found herself smiling. "Really, Dylan, there's nothing wrong with him."

That was the second quick flutter of anxiety he'd felt in less than minutes. He looked away and edged around the puddle to pick up pieces of what looked like a board game. Squatting, he reached for the playing pieces to another children's game that was strewn against a wall. Slippery from the soapy coating, one plastic piece shaped like a dog dodged his grip.

"You can throw that away," Chelsea told him, and felt anger surge when she noticed that the culprit had used a hammer on the polishing machine, denting the housing for the motor. "The board for the game is soaked." She pushed aside discouraging thoughts. No matter what obstacles she faced, she wasn't quitting. More than pride demanded it. She loved the business that she and Tess had begun, the work, meeting new people. She was no longer waiting for someone else's approval, no longer afraid of risks. She wrung out the mop in the bucket. Was that really true? Wasn't Dylan the biggest risk in her life?

"What do you use these for?" Dylan questioned.

She pulled away from her thoughts to see him sweeping an arm toward other damaged games scattered across the floor. "Nanny jobs. I found that kids respond better to me when I bring something they've never done before."

"Smart thinking."

"A survival tactic," she said with forced levity. While she finished mopping, Dylan headed to the outside garbage can. If Max stayed with her, she would have to make adjustments, hire someone to do nanny jobs. As Max got older, her work schedule might be more curtailed until he was school age.

Returning with the emptied trash can, Dylan saw her nudging a box across the garage floor to the wall. "Let me," he said, stepping close to take over the task. "What's in here?" he asked as he lifted the box. "Bricks?"

Chelsea shot a smile at him. "Gallon bottles of soap." She watched him move four more. "Was there a reason why you came by this morning?"

Dylan scanned the garage, nearly cleaned up. "To paint." *Logical excuse, Marek.* "If you can handle the rest, I'll get started."

"As soon as I'm done here, I'll help."

He rounded a grin at her. "Isn't a woman from your background trained to relax and let others do the work?" he teased.

Chelsea returned his smile before he left her alone.

She'd never been able to idle away time and watch someone else work. After finishing in the garage, she checked on Max. She was a step from his room when the phone rang. Her mother's familiar voice answered her greeting. Chelsea sought the closest chair. Some of her mother's calls went on endlessly. Today's message included praise about yesterday's party.

Chelsea had barely returned a thank-you when her mother said, "I called for another reason. I should be really miffed at you, darling." Despite her words, she spoke lightly. "I was flabbergasted when Elizabeth," she said, referring to her best friend, "told me your good news about the award." Her mother's voice rose with brightness. "It's quite an honor. When is it?"

Squeezing her eyes, she inwardly groaned. It took effort to push out a lie. "Mother, I don't really remember the date." Peripherally she caught Dylan standing in the doorway.

"Chelsea, that's absurd. You never forget anything."

"The award dinner is the same night as Richman's party," she admitted, because lying was virtually impossible for her.

"The same night as Richman's little gathering?" Her mother sounded so troubled.

The little gathering undoubtedly had a guest list of more than a hundred people. Wasn't this what she'd hoped to avoid? "Don't worry about it."

"But—"

"Really," Chelsea insisted. "There's no problem."

"Yes, all right, dear." To Chelsea's relief, some of

the concern had eased from her mother's voice. "But I want you to know how excited I am for you and Tess. This is a wonderful honor."

What could Chelsea say? She and Tess did feel honored, but family commitment had and would always come first to her.

Dylan heard her goodbye. Moving the roller along the paint tray, he knew the instant she joined him, but he didn't look back.

"You've done a lot already."

It had been impossible not to eavesdrop on the phone call. "You have a problem?"

Chelsea didn't chide him for listening. "My mother learned the award dinner is the same night as the political gathering for my brother." Her eyes ran over the well-formed muscles in his arms. "She'll be fretting now. I wanted to save her from feeling guilty about hurting my feelings."

He watched her dip the paintbrush in the can. "How would she do that?"

"Any time a woman has to make choices regarding her children, she feels guilty."

He believed that wasn't true of all mothers. "Guess you expect her not to be at the award dinner."

"Neither will I."

Dylan turned a baffled look on her. "What did you say?"

"I'm not going."

Dylan set the roller in the paint tray and moved near. Someone needed to talk sense into her.

"My brother has asked me more than once to be there. He wants to make the right impression."

Dylan read between the lines. "Of a close-knit family?" He didn't wait for her response. "What does that mean? One person sacrifices for the others?"

"You don't understand." Chelsea slapped paint at a door frame. "This is what I want to do. I'm not going to disappoint him."

Her cheeks were flushed from highly charged emotion. He couldn't relate to the dilemma. He'd always had to think of only himself. No one had ever aroused such unselfishness in him. For her family, she was giving up a night to bask in the glory of her achievement.

She brushed hair away from her cheek. "You think I'm wrong."

"I think families are overrated." Dylan couldn't look away from her soft eyes. All day he'd thought about being this near to her, remembered the way she'd felt in his arms. He only had to inch closer, and he could have what he'd wanted two years ago.

How hurt he'd been, Chelsea realized. "They aren't, Dylan." Her voice trailed off as he placed a hand on her cheek. Sensations hammered at her—the rough calluses, the heat of his fingers, the scent of him. Not breathing, she pressed a hand to his chest, and waited, but he turned away.

Confusion spiked through her. She wanted to be with him. She didn't expect romantic words from him. She simply wanted honesty. She knew she wasn't his type, but she had enough experience to know he wanted her. She was tired of being sensible, of listening to that voice in her head that insisted she never trust him again. She was tired of thinking of consequences. Here goes, she mused. Be brave. Or at least confident-sounding. "Let me make you dinner. A thank-you."

Dylan scowled at one of the freshly painted walls. Don't tempt me, he felt like yelling.

With his silence, all her courage withered away. By his silence, was he saying that he didn't want dinner or anything else with her? After all, he wouldn't be standing here now if it weren't for Max. She shrugged, wishing she could make light of the invitation. "It was just a thought." *Fool,* her mind screamed. She slapped the brush down on the roller tray. Once a fool, always a fool.

"I'll take you out for dinner." The words rushed out before Dylan had the good sense to stop them.

Chelsea angled a look at him. Dinner out. Was he asking for a date? "Max—"

"Get someone to watch him."

She turned; his eyes were on her, searching her face. "A baby-sitter?" She nearly rocked with the meaning behind his invitation. He didn't mean some family restaurant with high chairs, children's menus and crayons.

Dylan pushed the roller hard across the tray and soaked up the last of the paint. "I'll pay for whomever you get." He'd like an evening alone with her, a memory of a night with her attention solely on him. He'd had three others like that before he'd walked away from her. "We can go someplace nice."

We. She managed to keep a smile suppressed. She'd read his signals accurately. As her heart picked up a beat, she took a few deep, calming breaths. "I suppose Tess would watch Max."

Dylan avoided her stare by surveying the painted walls. "Good." With only window trim left, he gathered the roller and tray to wash them outside under the hose. "I'll wash these, and be back at seven."

"He asked you out?" Sitting on her sofa with her legs tucked beneath her, Tess gobbled on the chocolate bar in her hand. "Maybe he just wants to talk about something concerning Max." She corrected herself immediately. "No, he could stand at your front door and do that. This must be a date."

Chelsea smothered her excitement, aware Tess would offer sage advice until sensible Chelsea called off the date. "Would you take care of Max while we go to dinner?"

Curiosity still edged Tess's voice. "Sure, I'm not doing anything tonight."

Chelsea knew that wouldn't be true now that she'd shared today's earlier calamity with Tess. Tess would spend hours tonight pouring over the books to squeeze money from various places to replace equipment and supplies.

"Where are you going now?" Tess asked while balling up the candy bar wrapper.

Chelsea wanted to avoid a serious talk that would burst her bubble of excitement. "Home."

"Nope." Tess bounded to a stand, snagged her purse in one hand and grabbed Chelsea's arm with the other. "Pick up Max. We're going out."

Chelsea reared back enough to free her arm from

her friend's grip and reach for Max in his carrier seat. "Where?"

"Whether or not I think you're making a mistake, you're going to wow him tonight."

"But—"

"No buts," Tess ordered laughingly, with a hand on Chelsea's back while she urged her out the door. "You need a new dress."

"You should get a haircut, too," Tess suggested later when they entered an exclusive shop. "Make him hate himself for walking away from you." She snagged a dress from a display valet. "And put on makeup."

Chelsea frowned at the skimpiness of the first dress Tess handed her. "I never wear makeup."

"Okay. A little lipstick." She scowled as Chelsea placed the dress back on a rack. "What's wrong with it?"

"I don't like to wear red."

"No red," she repeated, as if filing the information. She swung a speculative look at Chelsea.

The smile made Chelsea nervous.

"Then this."

This dress made her feel even more uptight.

At five minutes to seven, she stood before her bedroom mirror with the new tube of lipstick Tess had thrusted at her. Despite Tess's groaning, she'd refused to apply the eyeliner and blush and all other cosmetics her friend had tried to suggest. With no knowledge at applying it, she would look like a Kewpie doll if she did.

With some hesitation, she slipped on the dress Tess had insisted she buy. Too much skin showed. Way too much. And it was too tight, wasn't it? She did a half turn in front of the mirror and sucked in her stomach. It was also too short. She would change, wear something comfortable, a sensible standby.

She never made it to the closet. At the sound of the doorbell, she jumped. She couldn't answer the door in this dress and then change. If she took the time to change first, he might leave. No, of course, he wouldn't leave, but—

Go, a little voice in her head insisted. Answer the door. Forget that dull, drab dress in the closet. A mistake or not, she rushed from the bedroom with her shoes dangling from her fingers. "Just a minute." Swiftly she wiggled her feet into the new sling-back heels, then opened the door.

Dylan couldn't stop staring, his eyes riveted to the hem of the ice blue silk dress that stopped just short of her knees. There were those legs again. "You look—" Capable of stirring any man's hormonal juices. "You look different." Instead of pinned or in that single braid, her hair hung loose, but not to her shoulders. "Your hair is different."

Self-consciously, she fingered the tip of a strand, still uncertain if she liked the new style that was fuller and shorter, cut to her chin and styled with wispy bangs. "I got it cut." Did he like it, hate it? Did he even care?

"It looks nice."

Nice. Was that good, bad, indifferent? She gave him a tentative smile. "Thank you," she said, assuming he'd meant the words as a compliment.

As she stood with her back ramrod straight, her hands tightly clenched, Dylan wished for magic words to relax her. Unable to resist, he reached out to touch the wispy strands of her bangs, then changed his mind. "Are you ready to leave?"

"Yes." It took courage for her to step away. Though the round neck of the dress scooped only slightly, the back dipped to a deep vee.

Breath swooshed from Dylan at the sight of her revealing dress. She really did look different. Sexy. He felt as if he'd been punched hard. She didn't need to do this. His gut already tightened whenever he was around her.

The candlelit restaurant offered a breathtaking view of the ocean. Moonlight shimmered on the dark water. Sitting across from her, Dylan considered the last time he'd dated her. Then, too, candlelight had played across her face, fascinating him. She looked even lovelier now.

Self-consciously Chelsea raised a hand to check the pins in her hair. None were there anymore. She fingered a strand of her hair. She shouldn't have gotten it cut. She probably looked silly. If she was having trouble getting used to her new look, then everyone else would, too. "This was a good idea," she said, to fill the silence between them.

Dylan looked over the rim of his wineglass at her.

"Why was it?" He hoped she would give him reasons, because he was having a hell of a lot of doubts.

"We can get to know each other better." He was staring at her, just staring. "That's good for Max." She wanted to slink under the table. Why had she even started this conversation? She looked down at the plate of food just delivered and poked her fork into the salmon. She'd been excited earlier, too excited, thinking of this as a date. But it wasn't, not really. Unlike some couples around them, he hadn't reached for her hand, hadn't even smiled at her.

"I thought you should know—" He paused as her eyes shot to him. Incredibly beautiful eyes. "I went to that lab a few days ago, the one you told me to go to for the DNA test."

Looking down, she hid a frown. She'd thought he'd gone before that. "So they have yours and Max's blood now."

"I was told it would take some time for the lab to have results."

Max. Chelsea frowned at her plate. She truly loved him as if he were a part of her, but she'd hoped for one evening, one hour when he wasn't the reason Dylan was with her. Silly thinking. The only reason she was sitting across a table from Dylan again was because of Max. "I thought you would do it sooner," she said, speaking her previous thought.

Dylan had been dragging his heels. He hadn't wanted to learn the truth, not really. The possibility he might be Max's father had scared the hell out of him. But in recent days, during a moment, a second, when he hadn't been aware, Max had become real, a human being with needs.

He'd also resurrected Dylan's memories of a lonely childhood, of years when all he'd wanted was for someone to care about him. He didn't want Max to ever know what he'd gone through. It had suddenly occurred to him that the only way to prevent that from happening might be if he learned he was Max's father. Then he could keep him safe, deflect the pain that so easily inched into a child's life because his parents didn't care.

Now, as he sat across from Chelsea, he reconsidered the idea. It didn't seem so great. How could he take Max from her? She loved him. She cared for him with all the tenderness and devotion of a mother. If he tried to do the honorable thing with Max, again he would be responsible for hurting her.

With his reticence, Chelsea wished for the evening to be over. She would never be witty with a gift for gab. She would never fascinate or charm a man. She would never appeal to an exciting man, because she lacked excitement.

She'd endured some terrible dates. This one ranked high on the list. Usually, even men bored with her company attempted to converse. Dylan had been so quiet that she'd wanted to kick him under the table.

Except for a few comments about the food, the meal passed in excruciating silence. Wishing for a quick end to the evening, she suggested they leave before coffee to pick up Max. After a silent drive to Tess's apartment, she hustled Max out the door. Fortunately, her friend was sleepy and asked no questions.

Though Max gleefully babbled when she fastened him in the car seat, he was snoring softly by the time Dylan carried him into the house later.

In the bedroom, Dylan lowered Max to his crib and mentally cursed himself. He'd wanted to give her a nice evening out. But when the waiter had materialized with their dinner, he'd decided not to let her get her hopes up. So he withdrew emotionally. If he took them to another step, if her feelings deepened for him, he could give her nothing in return. "It amazes me how he sleeps through anything," he said, not for the first time, when he joined her in the kitchen. That she wouldn't meet his eyes made the moment worse than he expected. "I guess I'll go now."

"You should."

The blunt two-word response brought his eyes back to her. Their gazes collided.

"Why did you ask me out?" Chelsea asked, wanting to understand how an evening that she'd thought held so much promise had gone bad.

Dylan cursed himself for lying to her. "Afterward, I'd planned to sleep with you." He watched color flood her face. "I changed my mind."

Chelsea straightened her shoulders. "You don't have to explain. You didn't choose me before, either."

Sure he had. But only he'd known that.

"And who said I would want to make love with you?" she challenged, turning away. She would open the door, and he could leave without more of a scene.

Dylan heard the hurt in her voice.

With the door open, she faced him and found him standing only inches from her.

"I wasn't offering anything that had to do with love." Whatever everyone's conception of that was. "That's why I changed my mind. Do you want a one-night stand, an affair?" He knew he should step back. She looked pale, vulnerable. He watched her moisten her lips, felt his blood pounding, and couldn't stop himself from doing what he'd wanted to do all night.

Touching her waist first, he moved his fingers to the edge of the dress and skimmed them up her naked back, then captured her mouth beneath his. He had only one thought. Kiss her until the taste no longer interested him. Touch her until the curiosity was sated.

As she parted her lips, he framed her face with his hand. Damned if he knew why he was doing this. But like a seduction, her fragrance enticed him. He closed a hand around her breast. For a moment he lost himself in the heat and softness of it.

Chelsea clung. She'd wanted this. Her heart thudded, promising to burst through her chest. As his lips demanded response, a mindless haze weakened her, and she gave in to aching need. *Dylan, it's me. Please know that it's me,* she prayed.

Chapter Nine

Heady from too much wine, she wondered if he needed that reminder. She wanted to close her eyes, let her body lean into him. A sigh slipped out as he nibbled at her earlobe. Tension made her feel so limp that she nearly sagged when he drew back. Why couldn't he lie with romantic words, save her pride, make her feel that maybe he'd made a mistake two years ago? If only he could pretend for a little while so she could have this one night. "Dylan, I know we wouldn't be together now if Max—"

"This has nothing to do with Max. Nothing at all." Tilting up her chin, he forced her eyes to meet his. Even as he wanted to be fair to her, he longed to drag her down to the floor with him. He couldn't do both. "It's about the way you look," he said, fingering a strand of her hair. "It's about not being able to walk away. It's about wanting you."

Breathless from his words, Chelsea gripped his arm. She couldn't let her fantasy slip away. This might be the only chance she would have with him, and for a memory she could cling to for the rest of her life. It didn't matter that she might face rejection later. She coiled her arms around his neck, hoping he never guessed the courage it had taken her.

Under his breath, Dylan damned himself. "You're too traditional," he said, as a reminder. "You think this means only one thing."

"You don't," she said a little breathy. "I know that."

She didn't understand anything. He would use her, take what he wanted, but never offer what she longed for, never give her the dreams she'd carried within her of home and family. She had to know that. "You're going to have regrets," he said softly, slipping his fingers into her hair.

She couldn't say she wouldn't, but she'd dreamed of being with him like this. "I never asked for any guarantees."

Dylan groped for control, tried to cool the heat searing him, but the scent of her, the slender body straining against him, invited. He couldn't resist. When her mouth pressed against his, he promised himself he would be gentle, careful. He felt her heart's frantic beat against his chest, and kicked the door shut as desire stormed him.

Pushing his tongue past her teeth and into the heat of her mouth, he heard her soft sigh. He wanted to savor. He wanted more. He wanted to make her ache with the wanting he'd carried with him for her.

His breath coming faster, he craved to drown in her sweetness. The scent of her enticed him. Her slender hands on his back beckoned him. The soft sigh that mingled her breath with his inflamed him. Running kisses over her face, he urged down the dress zipper and slid her dress off her shoulders. As the cloth shimmied down her hips, the silk whispered on the air.

He listened to her breaths quickening as he curled his hand under her breast, letting its weight and softness rest in his palm. He heard her sigh when he stroked her nipple with a slow, easy caress.

Pressing her against the wall, he traced the roundness of her breast with his tongue. Need whipped through him. He blocked it while he lowered his hands, tucked his thumbs in her panties to tug the last wisp of silk from her. With slow pleasure, he skimmed his fingers down and then up strong, slender thighs. He touched her with his hand, then tasted the same sensitive curves. She was sweet, wild, absorbing.

Drawing her down with him, he saw the heat of passion in her eyes, heard her soft moan of pleasure. He was beyond anything he'd ever felt before. He took his fill, his mouth moistening her flesh until she writhed beneath him. As if to bind them, her legs curled around his back.

A wave of emotion that went beyond passion floated over him. It had no name. He couldn't give it one. He tugged off his shirt. Buttons flew. It didn't matter. Nothing mattered but her.

When flesh finally met flesh, he lost all thoughts. He'd wanted to make her shudder. Instead, as her slender hand wrapped around him, she weakened him. If she'd asked, he would have given her anything she wanted.

Burying his face in her neck, he slid inside her on a low, breathless moan. Only the scent and heat of her skin filled his mind. She gasped, her body tensing, stilling him for a second. Then she sighed.

To stop, to even wait was impossible. He plunged deeper. Then they moved together, bodies arching against each other, moans mingling. She shouldn't trust him. Even now as he held her close, her body hot and damp against him, he prayed she never forgot that.

It was his last thought. Suddenly all that mattered was the sound of his name on her lips, and her shudder against him. Throbbing, he took her with him, giving whatever was possible, giving more than he thought he was capable of.

Dim morning light sprayed the room with warmth. Awake minutes ago, Chelsea searched every line of the face only inches from hers. Last night, she'd been his as she'd followed the command of his hands. She'd let her senses lead her, could still remember the moist caress of his tongue on her shoulder, skimming her body.

Never had she felt so free, her hands moving, touching every muscle of his back, the tautness of his

buttocks. Her face flamed even now as she recalled
caressing the maleness of him, stroking it, feeling the
pulsating.

Breathing had grown ragged as if as one they were
both gasping for the same air. A fury of need, no, a
frenzy had led them. She would never forget, never,
the moment when drugged by his taste, her heart hammering, he'd entered her, the heat and fullness of him
becoming a part of her.

Now with her arm draped across his stomach and
her head nestled against his shoulder, she felt him stir
beside her, and prayed all she felt wouldn't be
snatched away. "You're awake?" she asked softly.

"Yeah." Dylan remained still, his eyes closed.
During the darkness of night so much could be forgotten. Daylight broke the spell. It made everything
clearer. One thought returned, the same one that had
exploded in his brain before he'd fallen to sleep. He'd
been her first. He'd been the only man she'd known.
He wished now he'd been more gentle. He wished
that he'd known.

Would it have made any difference? Once she'd
been in his arms, he'd been powerless. Hadn't he
sensed that two years ago? It was one thing to desire
a woman. Passion rushed the fiery need. But to like
a woman, really like her, enjoy just watching her or
listening to her laugh complicated everything.

When the desire came, too, it tightened on him until he found himself in a battle against unbreakable
chains. He'd known, hadn't he, that he would feel like
this once he was with her? She'd brightened the dark-

ness within him. She'd made him feel strong, alive. He couldn't tell her any of that—not ever.

Chelsea nuzzled closer, her body still humming with excitement. "Last night was wonderful."

Dylan frowned at the crown of her head. Women placed a lot of importance on their virginity, didn't they? Romanticized that the man responsible for taking it was their one true love. "Why didn't you tell me?"

Raising her head, she angled a look up at him. He'd sounded—annoyed, angry—what? "I'm sorry if—"

He never let her finish, pressing a fingertip to her lips to silence her. "Never say that to me."

Her insecurities back in place, she wanted to hide from his intense stare. "I know I should have told you—" Heat swept over her face. "But you might have stopped." She'd disappointed him, hadn't she? Was that why he was upset with her? "I know I didn't know what to do."

With a fingertip, Dylan tilted up her chin. Softly, with a featherlight touch, he kissed her. "You did everything right," he murmured against her cheek.

Oh, she hoped so. "It really was wonderful for me."

As he caressed the sharp point of her hip, he buried his face in the curve of her neck. "You hardly have a lot to compare it with."

She sighed. "I thought I'd be a virgin forever."

Her bluntness surprised and amused him. Alone with his thoughts before she'd awakened, he'd worried about these moments, concerned she'd be serious and searching for words from him that he would never say. "Why?"

"I'm not the kind to make a man's heart pound."

"You're joking," he said, even more amused. Leaning on an elbow, he stared down at her and saw the seriousness in her eyes. She truly believed that about herself. "Did you feel mine? It was hammering. Why would you think that?" He needed no answer. Remembered words about how she felt because of her cousin flashed through his mind. How could such a competent, sensible woman allow another woman to make her blind to her own beauty?

As he dropped to his back again, Chelsea rested her head against his shoulder. "My father once told me that it was too bad I got cheated."

Dylan paused in stroking her shoulder. "Cheated?"

"In the looks department," she admitted awkwardly. "I was thin and gawky and had braces."

"How old were you when he said that?"

"Thirteen."

Anger—no, fury—sprang inside him with no warning. Damn that man. What a cruel and unjust thing to say to a daughter. "Do you look in a mirror and really see yourself?" Cheated? And she still believed that? "He was wrong."

Chelsea knew what she looked like. She was too thin, her hair straight, her nose thin, her mouth wide. She'd once stood in front of a mirror and had counted the freckles on her nose. Freckles belonged on little children. Women who turned men's heads had flawless, peach-colored skin.

Dylan drew her on top of him and pressed his lips to the tip of her nose, to the splattering of freckles. He wanted her to know what he saw when he looked at her. "You made me tremble," he admitted, because that was physical. It had nothing to do with feelings he didn't understand.

Lightly Chelsea brushed her lips across his. Because of the way he looked at her, he made her feel beautiful, more feminine, special. "Dylan, I did, too," she whispered.

He stroked the slender line of her thigh. "Did, too, what?"

"Tremble." Her breath caught as he rolled her with him.

"I know," he murmured before he scooted down, his mouth seeking her breast.

They barely had time to catch their breath when Max delivered his wake-up call. Her blond hair flying, Chelsea flew from the bed, offering Dylan a delectable view of her backside before she whipped on a robe. That image might burn within him through the day. As she shot out of the bedroom, he laughed and cradled an arm behind his head. If she'd stayed, he would have made love to her again.

Made love. Now, there was a phrase. What it really meant was sex. Good sex. Inexperienced as she was, she'd responded without inhibitions. She did something he never remembered any woman doing before. Instead of seeking her own pleasure, she'd tried to give it to him. Tentatively, even shyly she'd reached for him. And she'd made the blood boil within him.

Closing his eyes, he wondered if he stayed in the bed, if when done feeding Max, she would rejoin him. His body totally relaxed, he felt weightless. It had been years since he hadn't rushed from bed to start the day. And it felt so damn good.

"I'll start breakfast," she called out to him from the other room.

Reluctantly, Dylan nudged himself from the bed and tugged on his pants. Home, hearth, family mattered to her. Uncomplicated sex, no strings had always been his way. So now what? Wouldn't he complicate her life worse than before this time? No guilt trips. At least not right now. More than anything he'd ever wanted in his life, he wanted to enjoy this brief time with her.

He walked into the kitchen to see her on the phone. Pausing beside Max, he caught a whiff of an odor. He looked at Chelsea for help. Quiet, listening to the caller, she'd wandered to the coffee brewer. Now what? He couldn't just leave and ignore the job. Amused by his own dilemma, he lifted Max in his arms and stepped near Chelsea. When her attention shifted to him, he mouthed that he would change Max's diaper.

Chelsea cupped a hand over the phone. "I'm almost done," she assured him.

"I'll do it." He ambled toward the bedroom before she said more. A good father would change his baby's diaper. He wasn't too sure if he would be a good one in other ways, but he could do this much.

In the bedroom, he lowered Max to the changing table. Cooing, Max raised his chubby hand to him and wiggled his fingers to reach Dylan's nose. As Max's dark eyes studied him, so much emotion filled him that he thought he would burst with it. Bending his head, he kissed Max's forehead. *Little one, what are you doing to me?*

Chelsea was setting down the receiver when he wandered back into the kitchen. No matter where he was, if he smelled lavender, he would always think of the scent as exclusively hers. "You look stunned."

She couldn't believe what her family had done. As if it were as natural as breathing, she stepped into his arms. *Astonished* described the emotion she'd felt since her mother's phone call. "I can't believe what they did."

"They?"

"My family." She swayed back to rest against his arms.

Dylan tightened his hold on her. "What did they do?"

"They changed the day of my brother's get-together because of my award dinner. I told my mother that she didn't have to."

He noted a gleam of happiness in her eyes. "And what did she say?"

"'Of course we did.' She even called the governor."

Though his intention wasn't to droop her spirits, Dylan zeroed in on an obvious problem. "Was your brother upset?"

"I asked her that, too." She raised eyes filled with incredulity to him. "Richman suggested it."

He understood now why she'd looked so stunned.

They'd rearranged so much for her. An old agony
crept through him. When he'd been a kid, he'd ached
for a family, for that kind of love. Until this moment,
he hadn't fully understood that it was about give and
take. She'd been willing to let go of something important to her for them, and she hadn't lost anything.
"Sounds as if everything worked out."

"Not quite." Some of the hardest moments required nothing more than taking the first step. Her
heart, not her head, made her say, "I don't have a
date. Would you want to go with me?"

"Why would you want to do that?"

Chelsea stiffened. Maybe she was expecting too
much. Just because he'd slept with her didn't mean
he wanted the world to know they were together.
"You don't want to go?"

"That's not what matters." He wondered if she'd
considered others' reactions to them together. "More
important, do you really want me to go with you?"

"Do I—" It would be a public appearance of them
together. The same people she'd been humiliated in
front of two years ago would see them. Her heart
tugged at his consideration for her. "Yes." She stared
into intense pale eyes and remembered the gentleness
of his touch lingering on her body. *You're too trusting,* a little voice in her head said. She ignored it. For
better or worse, sensible Chelsea had disappeared
days ago.

Dylan ran a proprietorial hand down her hip. Sunlight streamed through the window onto her hair,
highlighting the reddish tone. Words had to be said.

He'd waited too long already. "I'm not good for you."

It seemed too late to remind her. "You've told me before. What are you afraid of?"

You. That boy. What you both can make me feel. Tangling his fingers in her hair, he brushed his mouth across hers lightly. Without hesitation, her lips parted, inviting him to deepen the kiss.

Chelsea felt her world tilt. She expected kisses from him as a seduction. But they were standing in the bright sunlight in the middle of her kitchen, and he'd still kissed her as if there were no other woman in the world.

In time, they would both know he wasn't the right man for her, Dylan reflected, even as he let himself capture this moment like others to memory. He would remember forever the warmth of the sunlight in the room, the scent of her skin, the way she felt so perfect in his arms.

It was nearly nine before Max was fed and dressed. While he played with the rings on the gym set in his playpen, Dylan finished off his third cup of coffee. By the stove, Chelsea flipped the omelet in the pan. "You didn't have to cook for me," he said when she was setting the plate before him, though he was glad she had.

"I like to cook." She saw his frown and matched it. "Is something wrong?"

"Aren't you eating?"

"Never breakfast," she said, breezing from the room.

Dylan released a low, throaty chuckle. This from the woman who'd chided him for eating a hamburger for breakfast.

He was finished and rinsing his plate when she reentered the room. He noted she'd slipped on one of those long dresses again that hid her legs. It didn't matter. His mind could visualize them. He'd seen every inch of her, felt the strength and slenderness of those legs.

"Will you lock up when you're ready to leave?" Chelsea asked as she poured formula into Max's bottles.

"Going somewhere?"

"I have to go to the shopping mall to buy a gift for a client."

Dylan drained the coffee in his cup. "Want company?" he asked nonchalantly, though annoyance was bubbling within him that he'd had to ask.

Chelsea swung a confused look at him. "You want to go with me?"

What did he have to do? Beg? "Do you mind?"

Worry sprinted through her. She'd heard a rougher edge in his voice. "No, I'd like the company."

"Fine." Don't get ticked off at her, he reminded himself. She has a legitimate reason to be cautious around you.

Avoiding his stare, she made much about zipping the diaper bag. "I didn't want you to think that I expected anything." She couldn't play games. Whatever her feelings were, she wore them openly. "I didn't want to bother you."

"Chelsea." She tensed when he took her shoulders.

Pressing his mouth to the crown of her hair, he held her close. "Bother me."

"Why doesn't this guy shop for himself?" Dylan asked later when they were entering the shopping mall. From the stroller, Max verbalized his pleasure with a new toy that Chelsea had attached to it.

"It's a gift for his wife."

Dylan had met executives who never took the time to purchase gifts for family. He'd always thought, why bother? Gift-giving should mean more than the exchange of token presents. "You're buying this gift for a client's wife?"

"It's one of the jobs I do," she explained simply. "I purchase wedding gifts and birthday presents."

He viewed that particular arrangement as deceitful. But the notion of her doing that seemed uncharacteristic. "Won't the wife think the gift was purchased by her husband?"

"Hardly. She knows I'm doing it."

Now he really was confused. "She knows what she's getting?"

"It wouldn't be right if she didn't know. It's too deceptive. Mrs. Caldwell is not only aware her husband asked me to pick up a present for her, but she called and described it to me."

"This makes no sense."

She smiled because he sounded so puzzled. "Why doesn't it?"

As she made a sharp right turn, he followed. "Why doesn't she buy it, then?"

"It wouldn't be from him."

He didn't know a thing about women, he decided. When she stopped, he lounged against the counter beside her and took in his surroundings. Instantly he decided that he should have paid attention to where they were going. Because he'd been playing follow the leader, he stood, the only male, in the middle of a lingerie department. He eyed a pale pink see-through outfit that was guaranteed to drive a man crazy.

"I forgot to tell you. My mother told me this morning that my aunt called from the airport."

It took effort, but Dylan gave up his fascination with a one-piece, silky peach number that had been draped across the counter. "So she's back?"

"Somewhere." Chelsea fixed a glare at the saleswoman. Mental telepathy failed. Her back to them, the young woman chatted on with a co-worker. "No one knows how to find her," she said, with a trace of the frustration she felt. "My mother didn't talk to her. She left a message with the maid."

He slid a thumb under a slip of a strap to dangle the silky peach cloth. "What's this called?"

"A teddy."

Faint lines crinkled at the corners of his eyes. "I like it."

Chelsea gave the filmy cloth a cursory glance. Her client's wife epitomized the stout, grandmotherly type. "It's too skimpy for Mrs. Caldwell."

He bent his head to whisper in her ear. "Not for you."

Chelsea tugged the teddy out of his hand. "I know my aunt paid off the lease on her apartment before leaving the country the last time, so I don't know which friend she'll be staying with.'' Her frown deepened. ''She said she would let my mother know.''

What Dylan could only interpret as distress wrinkled her brow. He caught her chin and forced her to look up. ''Want to share with me what's really bothering you?''

''I don't want to wait. One time my aunt mentioned a friend, an owner of one of those New Age stores. If I could find that friend, I might find her.'' She needed to know her aunt wouldn't rip Max from her.

''May I help you, sir?'' In her late twenties, the saleswoman suddenly delivered a smile at him that was meant to curl a man's toes.

He sort of grinned.

Chelsea cleared her throat for attention.

With real effort, the woman finally dragged her gaze from him. ''Yes, ma'am.'' As if Max had been invisible before, the woman's heavily made-up eyes suddenly darted to him. All flirtatious sexiness fled from her face.

Does she think we're a family? Chelsea wondered. The thought surged pleasure through her. She had a lot of dreams now, but she'd never abandoned the one about having her own family. That was as much a part of her as breathing.

Feeling Dylan's and the woman's eyes on her, she zeroed in on the business at hand. When she requested the demure-looking aqua peignoir that was hanging on a nearby rack in a size meant for someone bigger, the saleswoman sent her a puzzled look. ''It's a gift.''

''And this.'' Dylan held up the teddy by one strap.

"It's a gift," he said to the woman. He met Chelsea's look of disbelief. "It's for you."

"Dylan, I couldn't possibly wear that," she murmured out of the corner of her mouth.

She baffled him sometimes. For the world to see, she appeared a quiet, serious woman who blushed easily and gave tentative smiles. He'd seen other sides of her, the maternal one whose eyes sparkled with love when she looked at Max, the competent businesswoman who handled a stress-bound schedule with ease, and the lover who, with complete abandonment, had made him tremble like no woman had before. "I've seen you in less. Let me buy it for you, for me," he said softly. "On one condition."

With the soft seductiveness in his voice, her amusement waned. *Anything.* "What's that?"

"Wear it tonight."

Wasn't this all she'd been hoping for? More nights with him, loving him, feeling his hands coursing down her. "Tonight," she promised.

Chapter Ten

During the next week, Dylan became as much a part of Chelsea's life as Max was. She made them dinner; Dylan sent her flowers. They spent one evening in front of the television for an all-night marathon of Clark Gable films. They worked crossword puzzles, walked in the park, took Max on a picnic and went grocery shopping like a family. They made love in the middle of the afternoon and munched on crackers and cheese until Max announced he'd awakened from his nap.

Others might view it as a whirlwind romance. Chelsea cautioned herself against such thinking. Dylan had moments when he turned inside himself to distance her. Max proved more successful in reaching him. Every time Dylan held or touched him, changed his diaper or helped bathe him, the tie between them tightened.

A hectic morning, including a wait at one client's house for the roofer, meant Chelsea would arrive home late. As she was short one bottle for Max, he serenaded her during the last two blocks.

Zipping into the driveway, she saw Dylan's car parked at the curb. Last night, she'd given him a key to the house. As she expected, she walked in to the smell of paint.

By the sink, washing his hands, he sent her a questioning look because of Max's wail. "What's his problem?"

"I'm late with his bottle, and he needs his diaper changed."

"Max looks so sweet. Most of the time," he added as Max's squinched face reddened. "I'll sing if you promise not to." He lifted Max from Chelsea's arms. "Make a bottle," he said on the way to the bedroom. Confident now at diaper changing, he placed a gentle hand on Max's chest to hold him in place while he shook open the disposable diaper.

Max nixed all of Dylan's soothing attempts. Undeterred, Dylan whistled a medley of patriotic songs while unfastening the soiled diaper.

Fascinated by something new, Max stopped crying, his dark eyes fixed on Dylan's mouth.

Quickly Dylan used the damp wipes to clean him up, then slipped the fresh diaper beneath Max's bottom. With a foot in his mouth, Max gurgled with pleasure.

Standing at the doorway, Chelsea wished she had a camera. "Pretty pleased with yourself, aren't you?"

"He's not crying, is he?"

"Beginner's luck," she teased.

Over his shoulder, he narrowed his eyes at the too-bright smile on her face, a smile definitely there at his expense.

"Do you want to feed him while I check my answering machine?"

"That depends."

Chelsea darted an apprehensive glance at him. She was never quite sure how much to expect from him. "I can do it if you don't want to."

"I'll do it." Gathering Max in his arms, he followed her to the kitchen. With gusto, Max sucked at the nipple on the bottle. "What am I feeding him?"

Relaxing, Chelsea stepped close and fastened Max's bib. "Carrots."

Dylan held him until the bottle squeaked, signaling empty, then settled Max in his high chair. "Do you like carrots?"

Chelsea set a baby spoon and the dish on the high chair tray. A smile gently tugged at the corners of her lips. "Not particularly," she answered, speaking for Max.

Dylan scowled at the dish of orange mush. "I never liked green beans," he said, sounding empathetic.

"I won't make you eat them."

Hearing her soft giggle, Max swung his head in her direction, more interested in her than the spoon in Dylan's hand, and got a cheekful of carrots.

"Damn," Dylan muttered, and dabbed a napkin at

Max's cheek. The next spoon hit its target. The carrots went in Max's mouth and bubbled back out. Delivering one of his wide grins, he babbled something that sounded like "ma." Was that word for Chelsea? She would be thrilled if it was. "She gets to you, too, doesn't she?" he whispered, offering him another spoonful.

Behind him, Chelsea groaned at one of the messages on her answering machine. "Not the easiest of clients," she said, as an explanation to Dylan's frown.

The messages seemed endless to him. He counted twelve. On the wall near the phone hung a poster-size monthly calendar. Almost every day was filled with errands and jobs, some small like walking a family pet, some that should be overwhelming, like catering a party.

Finished jotting down one message, Chelsea looked back at them. With their dark heads bent toward each other, they looked right together. So where did that leave her? If he was Max's father, would he simply take him because he had the biological right? What about her? If only she could relax, enjoy, trust Dylan without question. "I think he's done."

The spoon scraped the bottom of the dish. "One more."

"Dylan, I wouldn't give him more," she warned.

As Dylan set the spoon close to Max's bowed mouth, Max sprayed the carrots back at him.

"Ah, Max." Dylan dropped his chin to his chest and viewed the orange specks on his shirt.

"I told you. When he's done, he's done." While Dylan wiped a damp cloth at his shirtfront, Chelsea took over cleaning up Max. Knowing his impatience level, she washed his hands quickly and dabbed the cloth around his mouth, then lowered him to his playpen, within reach of an activity gym.

Max verbalized with contentment. His bright-eyed gaze passed over the teddy bear dangling from a plastic ring and sought Dylan. Was Dylan aware of how often Max looked for him when he was in the room? Or that he kicked his legs and waved his arms with the excitement he felt?

"I have some errands to run, but I'll be back later," Dylan said as he rose from his chair.

Chelsea nudged herself from her thoughts. "Okay." She expected a quick kiss goodbye. Instead, his mouth captured hers as if impatient. Her head swam; she wanted to weep with the yearning she felt in his kiss.

"Goodbye," he murmured against her lips.

A touch breathy, she smiled. "That was some goodbye."

"Call it a celebratory kiss in advance," he said before stepping away.

She wasn't as confident as he was about tonight's outcome. With the award dinner that evening, she and Tess had cleared their calendars of jobs in the afternoon, deciding they deserved part of the day to lounge around.

A bundle of nerves, Tess called her within the hour and begged that she meet her for a quick lunch, anywhere. She needed someone to calm her down.

A short time later, with the midafternoon sunlight glaring in her eyes, Chelsea shifted from one of the hard benches to another at the outdoor seating area of a fast-food restaurant. Beside her in his carrier seat, Max's face squinched. He whimpered, a prelude to a wail for his bottle. Chelsea dug one from the diaper bag. "Shh, here it is." His little hands rose to grip the bottle she held for him.

"I got a large order of french fries to split with you," Tess said as she strolled out the door. She plopped on the bench next to her and dug out hamburgers. In between bites, Tess babbled with excitement about the evening's award dinner. "We probably won't win. Do you think we will?"

Chelsea dabbed a french fry in ketchup and smiled at her.

"I can't help it," Tess said about her exhilaration. "I've never won anything. Have you?"

"A spelling bee in fifth grade," she answered between slurps on a straw. She'd been so proud of that blue ribbon. To her credit, her mother had acted just as thrilled when she'd come home to show it off. Her father had been on the telephone. She remembered her mother making an excuse that he would see it later. Then Richman had dashed in with boyish delight about his riding lesson. For her brother, he'd stopped discussing business with a colleague; he'd beamed at his son.

"Chel?"

She snapped away a memory that was best forgotten. "What?"

"I asked if you want to get your nails done."

Chelsea sucked on the straw in her soda and shook her head. "No fake nails."

"Be adventurous."

Didn't that really mean taking risks? And hadn't she been doing that with her heart ever since Dylan had reentered her life? "I'd probably scratch Max with one of them," she offered as an excuse.

Tess's gaze shifted to him greedily pulling at the bottle's nipple. "Okay, no phony nails." She lifted the bun to peek at her hamburger. "I think they're skimping on cheese." She peered at Chelsea's sandwich. "Do you have much cheese on yours?" All morning, she'd hopped from one subject to the next.

Chelsea gave her a quick laugh. "Will you relax?"

"Can't. Pete," she said, referring to her husband, "says if we don't win, then he's gotten gray hair for nothing. I'm driving him crazy." She giggled and munched on another french fry. "Is your family coming tonight?"

To waylay any disappointment, she'd avoided mentioning the award ceremony whenever she'd talked to her family. She assumed they'd changed the campaign gathering date because Richman wanted her there to show family unity for his campaign. "They'll be too busy. This weekend is Richman's big gathering. There's always a lot of last-minute arrangements before a party. You know that."

Tess studied her for a long moment but said nothing. "Our appointments at the hair salon are at one." She checked her watch. "You'd better eat."

"Yes, Mother."

Tess's eyes brightened with laughter. "What's happening with Max's temporary daddy?"

"He's at a job site for the city's cultural center."

As Max finished his bottle, Chelsea lifted him from his carrier seat. Wide-eyed, he watched a flag waving in the breeze.

"What about tonight?"

"Pat-a-cake," Chelsea sang, bringing Max's hands together. "What about it?"

"Will Dylan be there?"

"Why would he be?"

"Come on, Chel." Curiosity colored Tess's voice. "Something is going on, isn't it?"

"Yes, he's going to baby-sit." He'd volunteered the other day, ending her hope that he'd come.

Tess swiveled a speculative look at her. "Is that all?"

Chelsea chose that moment to stuff a french fry in her mouth.

Despite her calmness when she'd been with Tess, Chelsea dealt with an attack of nerves while dressing for the evening ahead. She really doubted she and Tess would win the award. So many other women had admirably started successful businesses in the last year. But like Tess, she was thrilled at just being among the nominees.

"Would you zip this?" she requested, when Dylan arrived.

As she presented him with a view of her naked back, he gently pressed a kiss on her bare shoulder. "It's an important night for you." His lips brushed her hair when he tugged up the zipper.

"Maybe." That he'd arrived early surprised her. She'd seen the workload on the desk at his apartment.

He had to be playing catch-up. When she'd begun taking care of Max, she'd had days of arranging her work schedule around Max's eating and nap times.

"No jitters?" Dylan asked when she stepped away to wiggle her feet into her heels. She looked bright-eyed and vibrant in a black sleeveless dress that skimmed her knees. The excitement bottled within her darkened her eyes to the color of sapphires.

"Tons of them," Chelsea admitted. "But I have to pretend calmness. Tess is a wreck. Want coffee?"

More attuned to her than he realized, he perceived she was a bundle of nerves. A week ago, he wouldn't have noticed. "I'll get it."

With a last glance in the mirror, Chelsea toyed with her bangs. The light pressure of his hand on her back turned her in his arms. She sighed as much from the gentleness of his touch as from her emotions. Words clung to the tip of her tongue. Words she would never say because he wouldn't want to hear them.

"Good luck," he murmured against her lips. "If they're smart, you'll win."

She could have told him that she already felt as if she had. Just being with him, no matter how long that might be, offered memories she'd never dreamed of having. Memories she would cling to long after this was over.

In the hotel ballroom, silver gleamed and china shone on tables set with linen, crystal and fresh flowers. Silverware clattered, ice cubes clinked in glasses, voices buzzed with conversation. Sitting at one of the nominees' tables, Chelsea picked at each course of the meal. With coffee and dessert before her, she poked at the chocolate mousse.

Beside her, Tess scraped her empty plate. "Don't you want yours?"

Chelsea nudged her chocolate mousse toward her. "How can you eat so much? My stomach's revolted ever since we got here."

"I eat when I'm nervous. You starve yourself. Which is why," she said between mouthfuls, "you wear a size seven, and I don't." Her head swiveled to scan the ballroom filled with people. "I won't be catty, but did you see the one in the pink dress?"

"I saw," Chelsea answered.

"No, you didn't." Swinging her attention back to Chelsea, Tess grumbled, "Have you looked around at all?"

"Tess, I'm doing my best to appear serene." She'd learned the art of looking calm and composed. Often enough her father had scowled when she'd lost what he'd termed "ladylike decorum." Would he be proud of her this evening? He might make a show of it, but he would offer no hug in celebration, no joy for her, even if she won.

"You're doing an admirable job," her friend teased.

"So who is here that I missed seeing?" Chelsea asked, noting the presentation preparations beginning now that dinner was nearly done.

Behind her, a gentle hand touched her shoulder. She jumped and turned a look back to see her mother's approving glance over her black silk dress. "Mother!"

"Darling, you look lovely." Bending forward, she kissed Chelsea's cheek. "Did you think we'd miss this?"

The *we* reared her back. "We?"

With a sweep of her hand, her mother indicated a nearby table. Surprise rushed through her at seeing her brother.

The sight of another man shocked her. Dressed in formal black, Dylan stood near the open double doors that led in to the formal-looking room with its sparkling chandeliers. Another emotion swiftly snuck in. Panic. If Dylan was here, where was Max?

"We'll celebrate later," her mother said.

Chelsea dragged her gaze back to her mother. "We haven't won yet."

"Whether you do or not, we'll celebrate," her mother said, with an affectionate squeeze of her hand.

As she moved away, Chelsea's smile slipped. "What's he doing here?" she asked, indicating Dylan. Needing answers, she pushed back her chair to rise.

Tess seized her arm before she was halfway up. "Where are you going? It's almost time for the awards."

"I want to know where Max is."

"Sit." Tess's grip tightened. "Max is fine. After I left you, Dylan called me and asked if Mrs. Baines could watch Max," she said. "I knew you trusted her, so I set up the job," she whispered as the emcee introduced a speaker. "Okay?"

That didn't tell her why he'd decided to come.

"Why are you still frowning?" Tess murmured.

To calm herself, Chelsea sipped champagne from the fluted glass. "I didn't expect him to be here."

Tess grinned as if she'd discovered a secret. "I knew you were keeping something from me." She fixed her eyes on the podium, where the speaker was giving accolades for the nominees. "As your nearest and dearest friend, I'm aware your experience with men is limited, so let me tell you that men don't go out of their way to come to something like this unless they really care."

Chelsea resolved not to let Tess's words make her wish for something that would never be. He'd never said the word *love* to her. She couldn't let fantasy blur reality. "I can't afford to get that involved," she said, self-preservation in full force to prevent her from being too moved by his unexpected appearance.

Instead of concentrating on the speaker, Tess continued to frown at her. "You're worried, aren't you?"

"Yes." She was worried about having her heart broken. It occurred to her that despite all that had happened between them, her lack of trust remained. Nothing he'd done had obliterated the memories, the feelings she'd felt after his last brush-off.

Beneath the table, Tess suddenly gripped her hand, snagging her attention. "Here we go," her friend murmured, smiling pleasantly as if nothing overly exciting was happening.

Chelsea, too, focused on the reading of the nominees' names. A soft buzz circled the room. Then silence ensued. She thought it unbelievable that no one else heard her pounding heart.

What seemed like an eternity passed before the

speaker announced, "This year's award for Entrepreneur in a Small Business goes to Chelsea Huntsford and Tess Vanovitch."

The next few minutes blurred. Somehow, Chelsea managed to walk with Tess up to the podium without tripping, she made a brief speech without stammering, and she accepted congratulations. Craning her neck to see around the surrounding crowd, she never lost sight of Dylan.

She and Tess did a quick interview for a local businesswoman's magazine. Then, while Tess sought out her husband's congratulatory hug, Chelsea weaved her way past well-wishers to reach Dylan.

"She looks radiant," a voice said beside Dylan.

He met her mother's eyes. "Yes, she does."

Victoria touched his arm in passing, but Dylan hadn't missed the worry that had flickered in her eyes. He needed no psychic power to read her silent message. *Don't hurt my daughter.*

Earlier, while the nominees' names had been called, he'd seen Chelsea's tension in the tight set of her shoulders, imagined some of the uncertainty she'd carried from her childhood haunting her. Then, as others had gathered around her, he'd kept his distance. To join her in a room filled with women she knew would fuel gossip. He'd caused enough of that once before.

Beyond a sea of faces, her eyes locked with his. She would never believe him if he told her, but she looked beautiful. Slim, delicate. Her hair shone beneath the lights. Her eyes sparkled with the joy of the moment. Whether it was good for her or not, he couldn't stop himself. When she came within arm's reach, he drew her into the crook of his shoulder. "Congratulations."

Not caring who saw, Chelsea relaxed against him. "It's been a night of surprises." She was aglow from the happiness and recognition of her accomplishment. "You didn't tell me you were coming."

"I decided I wanted to be with you," he said honestly.

Tonight, or always? Cowardliness kept her silent. For now, for this moment, everything in her life seemed so right.

Dylan withdrew his arm from around her. "I'll see you at your house."

Chelsea grabbed his hand. "Celebrate with me."

"I'd hoped you'd ask."

Chapter Eleven

Midmorning raced in on them. Chelsea nibbled on a cracker and surveyed her new home office. Earlier, she'd had a desk delivered. With Dylan's help, she moved in furniture from other rooms, including a wicker trunk, a settee and a cabinet for supplies. "I love this room," she said, tossing several pumpkin-colored throw pillows on the settee with its beige cushions.

"What kind of schedule do you have today?" Dylan asked, waiting for the final hiss of the coffee brewer.

Chelsea shook her head. "None." Since Max's arrival in her life, she'd planned her schedule to keep at least one day free each week. "Do you?"

Relaxing didn't come easily to him. The result of too many years when he'd worked his tail off in construction to learn a trade, to get somewhere. He'd already known what it was like to be nowhere. Often considered a workaholic, he'd stayed at the office past midnight and on holidays, working on bids, studying architectural plans. He'd had nowhere to go, no one special to be with.

But until minutes ago, he uncharacteristically hadn't given a thought to the stack of work at the office or on his desk at home. "Meetings. But let's do something, anything you want this evening. Could you get someone to watch Max?"

Chelsea rounded a look on him. "What do you want to do?"

Her pleased look moved him. "You name it."

"A movie?" She rarely had time to go to them. "I love the buttered popcorn."

He returned by six that evening. Together, they made dinner. Chelsea grilled hamburgers while Dylan chopped cabbage for coleslaw. The domestic scene spiraled a fantasy through her. Dozens of warnings were futile. An undercurrent of excitement danced through her as her mind flooded with what-ifs.

With the dishes done, she cleaned up the kitchen. On the floor, Dylan zoomed Max's soft stuffed car past him, stirring Max's giggle. It was a memory she would tuck away forever.

Apologizing, the baby-sitter arrived late. Somehow Dylan avoided a speeding ticket, and they arrived at the theater with minutes to spare. Even before the opening credits ended, they'd finished half a bucket of popcorn.

She was content, maybe too much so, Chelsea acknowledged as she rested her head against his shoulder. But tonight she didn't want to think so much, didn't want to let doubts spoil what she had now. She accepted that this might not last, but she was content to just be with him, and for now she would forget about future promises.

"Want more popcorn?" he whispered during a moment of tension-setting music from the speakers.

"I'm stuffed." As she returned her attention to the screen, she gasped when the heroine slipped from the top of the elevator shaft and dangled, clinging to the hero's iron-grip.

Dylan closed his hand over hers. She clasped it tightly through the movie's scene. She made him feel as if he didn't have a care in the world. In the dark theater, he draped an arm around her shoulder and dipped his other hand into the oversize bucket of popcorn she held.

He'd never spent an evening like this. In his youth, he'd never had time for necking with some girl at the movies. Even before his sixteenth birthday, he'd worked, lying to get a job at a small grocery store where the owner had cared less about how old he was and more about him having the strength to haul in crates of produce and chunks of ice. Being lazy or irresponsible never had been an option. Being enchanted with a woman had never been in the game plan.

"That was so good," Chelsea said, while credits rolled and she stood with Dylan to leave the theater.

Dylan gave her a wry grin. "Like being scared?"

"I wasn't scared."

"You numbed my fingers."

"Did I really?" she asked with a look of alarm.

His laugh answered her.

Chelsea pulled a face at his tease. "You—" Playfully she jabbed at his arm.

As they neared his car, he slid his arm around her waist again. He wasn't ready for the evening to end. "Can you roller skate?"

Her laugh rolled out. "Roller skate?"

She was still laughing when she was lacing the skates he'd rented for her at a nearby rink. "This could be an experience to remember."

Deftly, he crisscrossed his laces and tied them, then drew her to a stand with him. "You're probably a great skater."

Another laugh bubbled in her throat. Her gaze fixed on her feet, she gripped his arm and shuffled forward with him. "I'm not." She squealed as her feet chose opposite directions. Before they'd glided around the rink once, she nearly took him down with her twice. "It's not fair that you're so good at this."

"Be grateful I am." Dylan grinned.

"I am. We're lucky. Very lucky. Or we'd both be soothing sore backsides in a warm tub tonight."

Dylan thought the idea had merit. "Want to pretend and do that, anyway?"

Chelsea dared a look away from her feet. "Is that your version of the 'come see my etchings' line?" she teased.

He cocked a brow. "Is that the line some guys give you?"

Looking down, she concentrated on her feet. "Not me." No man had ever tried to seduce her to his apartment. She'd had a few adolescent necking sessions with boys as shy as she'd been. But their fumbling efforts had cooled her ardor quickly.

"For the record..." Abruptly, he stopped her with him.

Swaying on the skates, Chelsea clutched at his shirt. "Don't do that. Don't stop like that," she reprimanded him lightly.

He met her sparkling eyes. Even during light-hearted moments, she touched him in a way no other person ever had.

"What were you saying?" she asked, steadier now with his hand firm at her waist.

"For the record, no woman has ever been at my apartment, except you."

"Lauren—" Her cousin's name slipped out before she could stop it.

Dylan mentally winced. He wished he and Lauren had never been. "Not Lauren, either. You're the first."

The first. All her life, she'd come in second to other people.

Cupping her shoulders, Dylan stooped slightly to put his face in her vision. "It's still early."

She thought he needed a reminder. There wasn't just the two of them to consider. There was a baby at home. "Dylan, the baby-sitter—"

"I'll pay her extra." He felt her weight against him as she leaned for support. "I'll have you home by

midnight.'' He kissed the tip of her nose. ''I promise.''

Heat churning within him, he kissed her in the un-
derground parking lot, he kissed her again in the elevator on the way to his apartment. His body heating,
he wanted her now. Another kiss at the door nearly
weakened him. Straining against him, she twisted her
lips across his, her tongue matching and dueling with
his.

But showing more control than he felt, she put her
hands to his chest to ease him away. ''The keys,'' she
said, between needed breaths. ''Open the door.''

Surprising himself, he fumbled with the key. Behind him, he heard the muffled ring of her cellular
phone. ''Don't answer it.''

Resisting it was impossible. Gathering her wits,
Chelsea tugged the phone from her purse. ''A call
this late has to be important.''

Mentally, Dylan grumbled while he nudged her
into his apartment. Giving her time alone to answer
the call, he wrestled with impatience and ambled to
the refrigerator for a bottle of wine he'd kept for an
important occasion. By the time he rejoined her, she
was jamming the phone back in her purse. Dylan set
the bottle and the glasses on a table. ''Was it the
baby-sitter?''

She gave him a quick, reassuring smile. ''No, a
client. Her aunt needs to be picked up at the airport
tomorrow morning.''

Pouring the wine, Dylan curbed the desire sim-
mering within him as he saw the worry that had

clouded her eyes for a second. Near her, he skimmed his hand down her arm.

"The call made me think about my aunt Marlin. I'm nervous about what she'll say," she admitted, because sharing thoughts with him was becoming as natural as breathing. "I keep thinking of reasons why my aunt shouldn't want Max. Then when I look at him, I think how precious he is. Of course she'll want him. She's his grandmother."

"You make it sound so simple. But just because she's his grandmother doesn't mean she's the right one to raise a child."

Chelsea wondered if he was talking about himself now. Before, she'd counted on him having doubts he could raise Max. "You haven't made any decisions yet about Max?"

"Today I have no right to. Tomorrow might be a different story." Dylan pivoted away to reach for the wine glasses. "If I were you, I wouldn't worry so much about Marlin. Not every mother or grandmother is maternal."

He'd sounded cold. Bitter. This wasn't about Max, Chelsea sensed instantly. "Why do you say that?"

"It's obvious, isn't it?" Unexpectedly, old pain seemed a breath away. He handed her a wineglass, but with her eyes on him, searching, he failed to block the explosive memories. "Because it's true." A challenge instinctively rushed forward. "Lauren wasn't maternal, or she wouldn't have left Max."

"Lauren loved him," Chelsea said in her cousin's defense, because she believed that to be true.

A hardness edged his voice. "She didn't love him enough to stick around."

Chelsea couldn't argue, as she felt his tension. She closed the space between them and gently touched his arm, wishing to take some of the pain she saw in his eyes. "Lauren isn't what this is about, is she?"

"Forget it."

As anger snapped in his eyes, Chelsea reared back, feeling as if he'd slammed a door. Hurt rose within her. He'd been intimate with her, but yet again he was pushing her away from what he was feeling. The hurt was her own fault, not his, she reminded herself. She knew he didn't want anyone to get too close. He'd told her that he liked short-term relationships. Shallow ones, she assumed now. "Maybe I should go."

If she'd prodded, pushed, insisted, he could have resisted her. But he'd seen that familiar uncertainty flash to her face. In his own way, he was rejecting her. And, dammit, he didn't want to hurt her like that. She'd already endured her share of anguish at the hands of a father who'd lacked even a smidgeon of sensitivity for his own daughter. "Chelsea—"

She stilled before reaching for her purse.

"There's not much to say," he offered as an explanation. "I had bad feelings about my mother. You know that."

"But you included your grandmother when you said that, didn't you?" She treaded carefully, aware that emotions were teetering close to the surface. "I don't know why you would. You can't reasonably blame her for dying."

"Didn't die," he murmured, then turned away.

She'd heard him and still needed him to say more, to clarify. "What?"

All that he'd thought he'd buried years ago rose as if someone had scraped away the layers of anger and pain covering it. "She didn't die."

"But you said—" Confused, she inclined her head, wanting to see his face better. "You said you were in foster homes for years."

"What's so hard to understand?" He drilled a cutting look at her. "Read between the lines. My grandmother didn't die when I was a kid." Weariness weighed him down. Talking about it hurt as if it had happened yesterday. "She claimed she couldn't take care of me. That's what I was told after she left me with social services to be placed in foster care."

Had he believed he was abandoned? "If she was old, Dylan—"

He sensed the excuse coming. "She wasn't old. She was forty-three years old. And bitter," he said with more hardness. "Bitter toward men in general because one had left her, and one had ruined her daughter's life."

More tired than he realized, he ran a hand over his eyes. "She didn't even play fair. If she had given me up for adoption, I might have found a family. But she didn't. So the best they could do was place me in foster care. It didn't pay to get too happy, too comfortable." He shrugged with indifference, but he recalled one foster home.

To a nine-year-old, it had seemed as good as heaven. The air had carried the scent of hay just cut and the sounds of animals—a rooster, cows, the family dog. He'd liked the farm, and the family. Inside the house, it smelled of fresh-baked pies. A woman named Katherine, whose smile lit up a room, had seemed to care. There had been three other foster children plus their own baby. The kids all had chores to do. That was a rule: chores, then homework. And they all rushed to get them done, because every night while dinner cooked, her husband entered the kitchen, washed his hands, then hustled all of the kids outside to play baseball or kick ball. His name was Joe. That was a memory he could remember. Some others he preferred to forget.

"The older I got, the more difficult I was. I knew people were being paid to take me in. I figured they should work for that money." He didn't want to talk about it anymore, ever again. He didn't want to think about it.

Chelsea's heart twisted. For a child, no pain surpassed rejection by a loved one. "Dylan?"

"Save the sympathy."

Instead of pushing her away, his hurt radiated to her. "No sympathy." All her life she'd shied from taking chances, wanting so badly to win one man's approval, and she never had. Chelsea pressed her forehead to his. When he didn't pull away, she slid her arms around his waist and gathered him close.

Torn between the softness she drew out of him and anger with himself for telling so much, he stayed near her. "What do you want from me?" he asked against her hair.

"To know what you feel."

He hadn't realized how much he'd needed her touch until he felt the heat of her hand at the back of his neck. No one, he realized, had ever said that to him. He wanted to pull back from the moment. It weakened him. It made him feel. Long ago, he'd learned to block the anger and pain, to feel nothing. Now he couldn't. The arms around him tightened. He'd been held by other women as a prelude to sex, but not like this, never like this. This comfort wasn't something he'd ever looked for from anyone. He couldn't resist it, because for the first time in his life, he didn't feel alone.

Chelsea closed her eyes as his arms came around her. Her heart open and caring, she blocked niggling concerns about where emotions for him would lead her. All that mattered was him, his feelings. She wanted to do something to give him time to forget, to find peace.

Her face inches from his, she searched his eyes. They looked fierce, but she knew the softness in him, knew his gentleness with her, his tenderness with Max. This moment wasn't about needs or desire. It was about giving, simply giving all that was conceivable to another person, even if only for a little while.

Her scent curled around him. Her softness soothed him, not just the softness of her flesh, but the softness within that made her special. With a generous heart, she'd reached out and touched him. "I want you," he murmured against her mouth. Suddenly all that mattered to him was this moment and tasting her sweetness everywhere. Slipping his hand in her hair, he held her face still and lowered his mouth to hers. "Are you staying?" he asked softly.

"I hope so," she barely managed to say, as his fingers began deftly loosening the buttons on her blouse. In one swift move, he slid it from her shoulders to let it slither down.

Chelsea moaned. The need building within her exploded as his knuckles brushed her flesh while he pushed wispy silk away. Growing hungrier, she yanked at the buckle of his belt. Her breath caught as he tucked his thumbs into the top of her panties and his fingers slid them downward. Closing her eyes, she swayed toward him, and floated on the caress of his hand down her body. She was beyond the uncertain woman he'd first made love with.

Her body matched the tension she felt in his as it strained against hers. Her hands moved down his bare back, her fingers inched beneath the waistband of his pants. Even as he drew back to free himself of them, her mouth remained on his, twisting across his lips, seeking the warm recesses of his mouth, drawing in his breath. His moan thrilled her. With awe, she knew now she held the power to weaken him just as he did her. Naked, pressed tight to him, her blood pounding, she backed up the few steps to the sofa.

Her body heating, she sighed as his mouth traced a path down her throat. Her pulse thudded as his strong hands glided slowly across her breasts, down her belly, between her thighs.

He murmured something, unintelligible words. She didn't need to hear them. Breathless, she was lost in a fury of need. Her hands coursing over him, her heart hammering, she shifted, lowering her lips to his rib cage, pressing them to the sharp point of his hip, tracing the rock-hard muscle in his thigh. Pleasure came on a rush with the sound of his low moan. The smell and taste of this man who was a part of her made her gasp as his fingers gripped her buttocks, and he rolled her to the floor with him.

With his hard thighs pushed against hers, and his warm belly heating hers, she clutched at his shoulders. Breaths ragged, her legs curled around his back, she squeezed her eyes shut and raised her hips to meet him, to seek the pleasure awaiting her once more. And journeyed with him wherever he wanted to go.

It was nearly midnight when she made a quick phone call to the baby-sitter, promising that she was on her way home. Dropping the portable phone to the bed, she rushed to the chair near the door. On it, Dylan had tossed her bra and blouse. She found her panties under his shirt. "I had a wonderful time tonight."

Dylan stood up. He had, too, though he wished he hadn't poured out feelings he'd thought were long forgotten. "I owed you one."

Her fingers paused on a button of her blouse, Chelsea raised her eyes to him. He stood resplendently naked before her.

"Our last date stunk," he explained, while yanking up his jeans. At her silence, he cracked a grin. "You could have protested." He heard her giggle while she wiggled into her jeans. Staring at her as she slid on shoes, he wished for some way to make everything right for her. "I've tried to get you out of my system," he said, speaking his thought.

His unexpected serious tone stilled and tensed her. What woman wanted to hear that? Had he deliberately offered that as a warning to keep her from feeling too much? Uncertain suddenly, she pivoted toward the mirror to brush her hair.

In the mirror, Dylan saw the sadness in her eyes. Instinct told him that he wasn't making what would come later easier, but when she was so near, she chipped away at his sensibilities. He couldn't leave her alone. She mattered too much. Moving behind her, he touched her shoulders. "It's up to you. I'll back off now if you want me to." He needed her to push him away, because he couldn't find the will on his own.

Life was suddenly far too complicated, Chelsea decided. She wasn't a foolhardy woman. Or at least she never used to be, but how would she assess a woman who'd been hurt once and had dived back into a relationship with the same man? "Do you want to?"

"If I could stop, I would," he said honestly.

The admittance bordered on commitment. Don't misinterpret, she warned herself. Already he looked as if he regretted saying that. But it pleased her. She laid her head back on his shoulder. "I don't expect more than this," she assured him, and closed her eyes as his arms wrapped tighter around her to hold her against him.

Staying at her house had seemed right, natural to Dylan.

Chelsea had left an hour ago to run to a local bakery to get a cake for a client. At dawn, she'd bounded from the bed, muttering to herself about oversleeping. She'd tugged on a sweatshirt and jeans, and wiggled bare feet into sneakers before offering him a back-handed wave.

When she returned, he was nursing a morning cup of coffee. Appearing less frazzled, her hair less mussed, she gave Max a quick peck on the cheek.

Dylan set a bowl of oatmeal for Max in the micro-wave. "Did you get the cake to your client in time?"

Hunkered before Max, she walked her fingers across the high chair tray and sung "Itsy-Bitsy Spider" to him. "The poor woman has her hands full."

Dylan laughed as she rolled her eyes.

"She had a sleepover for her daughter's eleventh birthday." She snatched up her shoulder bag from the chair she'd tossed it on. "Twenty jubilant and ener-getic preadolescent girls were screeching and giggling when I walked in with the cake." Sidling close, she kissed him quickly, then scooted away. "I need to change," she said, before disappearing into the bed-room.

Behind Dylan, in his high chair, Max banged plas-tic spoons against the tray with a steady rhythm.

With the ding of the microwave, Dylan took out the bowl and added milk to the cereal, then blew at the oatmeal, hoping it cooled before Max's patience level dropped. He didn't mind this task as much as the diaper changing, though he did both without grumbling now. "Just a few minutes," he promised while opening the freezer. He plunked an ice cube in the steaming cereal and stirred it several times before he tested the temperature against his lips. No way was he eating any.

"Looking good," he said to Max, and received a gleeful gurgle as a response. Once more he tested it before he offered Max a spoonful.

Max continued to bang the spoons while Dylan fed him. He sputtered every other spoonful of the oatmeal from his mouth. "Back in, big guy," Dylan urged, scooping the oatmeal from his small bottom lip, and offering the spoon again. Smiling, he touched the top of Max's head. Precious. Chelsea had called him precious. He was important to her, and to him. The kind of life he might lead might be out of Dylan's hands. "I hope it's a good one. But what if I can't help make it that way?"

He stilled, holding the spoon in midair. Why couldn't he? Why did he have to bow out if Max wasn't his? He could take him to ball games, teach him to swim. He could do more, too.

Leaning back in his chair, he kept feeding Max with one hand while he reached with his other for the phone on the counter behind him. In need of his lawyer, he quickly punched Alex's home phone number.

"I need to come in to your office tomorrow," Dylan said after his friend's greeting.

"I don't know what time is open. I'll check with my secretary," Alex mumbled on a yawn. "What do you want done?"

Dylan grimaced as Max's fingers plunged into the oatmeal. "I want you to set up a trust for Max."

"Max? Oh, the baby," he said before Dylan answered. "Give me a minute here. Do we have to do this tomorrow? You don't even know yet if you're his father."

Dylan swiped a finger at the oatmeal on Max's soft cheek. "No. I want you to do it now."

"Now?" Sounding more awake, his friend had taken on his lawyer's tone.

"It doesn't matter if I'm his father or not. I want the trust set up for him."

"You want…?"

"I'll see you tomorrow, Alex," Dylan said to his friend, and set the receiver back in its cradle. Leaning forward, he wiped the oatmeal off Max's fingers. Whatever happened with Max, in some small way, he would be a part of his life now.

He'd needed to do something, he realized. If Max was his, all he'd believed before about no marriage, no family wouldn't have mattered. He would have a son, a family.

Before he had thought he was content. He had his business, friends and female companionship when he wanted it. But he'd had nothing. It had been an empty life because he'd had no one he'd cared about. And there had been no one who'd given a damn about him.

He'd thought he'd gotten used to that life. It had been the one he'd known since childhood. But he felt different today. The hostility, the resentment that he'd carried with him through his childhood had vanished.

Why? He'd wondered about that earlier. Only one answer rang true. Chelsea. Last night when they'd talked openly, there had been nothing sexual about her embrace. She'd simply offered unconditional support. He'd never had anyone he could depend on, anyone who'd be there for him, until her.

He'd never wanted to keep someone in his life forever—until her.

Did he really want to? Was this love? *Love.* He straightened from his thought. He'd never expected to even think it. Was he in love with her? How long had he felt that way? He had no answer. He only knew he wanted to be with her. He liked seeing her smile, hearing her laugh. He liked holding her in his arms at night and waking up in the morning to find her beside him. He wasn't ready for another goodbye. He was tired of all the goodbyes he'd endured in his life. Damn tired of them.

He'd found a child who needed a home as much as he had. He'd found a woman who made him feel complete, the one he wanted to build a life with.

Dylan blew out a long breath. Swell. Now what? What did he do now? Would she believe him? He'd rocked Chelsea's world once. He'd been a heel before. Oh, he could pretend he'd been doing something noble, stepping away before she got too attached to him. But he'd been running from her. Maybe, even two years ago, he'd sensed that if he'd spent more time with her, then he would have to face that. So he'd pretended he was trying to be fair with her. He hadn't wanted permanency, he'd thought. But he did want it; he wanted everything with her. And he had no idea how to convince her that this time he wouldn't walk away.

"I'm ready to go," Chelsea said, breezing into the room.

"Go where?"

In the bedroom, she'd taken a moment to call her mother. As undependable as ever, her aunt hadn't shown up yet. Impatient, Chelsea had resolved to take matters into her own hands. She made a suggestion to Dylan. Silent, he frowned, even though he nodded agreeably.

Dylan thought what she wanted to do amounted to a wild-goose chase. Trying to locate a store owner, Marlin's friend, seemed doomed for failure, but he'd humored Chelsea about going to the New Age shops that Marlin was known to frequent.

In a short time, he'd learned one thing about the smiling woman standing before him. If any possibility existed that she could do something about a situation, she would plunge forward rather than sit and wait for results.

He'd spent weeks doing that in regard to Max. At first, indecisive about what he would do if he learned he was a father, he hadn't been anxious for an answer. Now he still wanted the results to take forever. But his reason was different. He didn't want what he had found with the boy to end.

Unlike Chelsea, he wasn't as optimistic that Marlin would let her have Max. The idea of the three of them together as a family bordered on perfect. Too perfect. Life had never been that good to him.

Inside one of the stores, Max sat in his stroller, transfixed by a huge spinning hexagon that was suspended by a string from the ceiling.

Its hypnotic rotations bothering *her,* Chelsea pivoted the stroller in a different direction.

At the store's high counter, Dylan whipped out a photograph of her aunt Marlin. "She might be a regular customer, or used to be. She's been out of the country for a while."

Dressed in a multicolored caftan, the man stroked his salt-and-pepper goatee. "Don't know her."

Chelsea received Dylan's frown. Four other shop owners had uttered the same comment. "I know I'm not wrong about this," Chelsea insisted as they ambled toward the exit. "My aunt was always talking about scrying, about a friend who owned a store."

"Scrying?" His brows knitted with a frown. "Do you know what that is?"

"I'm not sure." Chelsea pushed Max's stroller outside. "But it has something to do with a glass of water." She shrugged. "More important to me is why doesn't anyone know her?"

Dylan shared a similar thought. The times he'd encountered Marlin at Lauren's apartment, she'd spouted off what had sounded like mumbo jumbo to him. "Could be we're in the wrong part of town," Dylan speculated.

"This is the closest area to what used to be her home before she left for her trip abroad."

In response to a red light, he slipped a palm under her elbow to stop at the corner. "That's logical, but I remember her. She always leaned toward the absurd."

"We'll have to look somewhere else," she insisted, not wavering in her determination to find that friend.

Weary from what he viewed as a morning wasted, Dylan motioned toward a restaurant across the street. "Let's stop for something to eat over there."

The idea appealed to Chelsea. Though she'd worn sandals, her feet screamed for a rest after all the walking. She preceded him into a restaurant decorated like a five-and-dime diner and crossed the floor with its black-and-white-tiled squares. Ahead of them, a waitress wearing a circular felt skirt with a poodle embroidered on it showed them to one of the red vinyl booths.

Dylan's gaze met hers over the top of the paper menu in his hands. "What do you want to eat?"

"A chocolate milk shake," she said to him, and nearly jumped when the waitress suddenly materialized to take their order.

"Anything else?" she asked, looking unenthusiastic about her job.

"A hamburger with loads of onions."

"Make it two." To ease her troubled look, Dylan teased her after the waitress left. "That's better than what you ordered the other night," he commented.

She looked down to hide a smile.

He paused and narrowed his eyes as if trying to visualize the Japanese words he'd read on the take-out menu. "What was it called?"

"Sashimi moriawase."

"Yeah, that," he murmured. "Whatever it was."

"An assortment of sliced raw fish." Catching his grimace, she looked away, grinning.

Because touching her came naturally now, he closed his hand over hers resting on the table. "For your brother's sake, wouldn't your aunt show up tonight at your mother's house for Richman's big gathering?''

"My aunt never worried about appearances. She won't be there. She never came to family occasions.'' Mostly because of her father's censure, Chelsea recalled. "Are you still going with me?''

That seemed fair. "I'll endure it, since you agreed to go with me to a company picnic.''

"You asked me when I could barely breathe, much less think,'' she said, reminding him of the other night and their long, leisurely lovemaking.

"Smart of me, wasn't it?'' As far as the picnic he had to attend, he didn't plan to stay long at it; he never did.

"Hmmm, good,'' she murmured to Max. Again she dipped her straw in the milk shake, and then stretched toward the stroller to offer Max another taste. With gusto, he sucked on the milk-shake-coated straw.

"Who's going to watch Max tonight?''

"Tess is baby-sitting. She said that I could bring him by early. I was glad she volunteered to watch him.'' A smile curved the corners of her lips.

"What's so funny?''

"She said that she hoped her husband Pete found the presence of a little one inspiring. Her biological clock is ticking, and she claims she is definitely ready for motherhood.''

"Is that how you feel?''

The question surprised her, because he usually kept talk about families at bay. "I didn't think about being a mother until Max came into my life.''

Dylan had to ask. "You didn't hear that clock ticking?"

"It doesn't matter if I did or not. I couldn't marry someone I don't love just to have babies."

If he wasn't Max's father, she would get what she wanted. She might get her baby. Would she want him, too? He'd been stalling.

It took courage to ask a woman to commit forever to one man. Old feelings of rejection still plagued him, he knew.

Chapter Twelve

Dylan nudged away more serious thoughts. He couldn't pop the question yet. For as much as everything seemed perfect between them, trust developed at an excruciatingly slow pace. He wasn't sure he'd convinced her yet that hurting her again was something he would never do.

When done with lunch, they spent time on a nearby park bench while Chelsea fed Max his bottle. With him babbling, she pushed the stroller into another shop.

Two women, wearing long gypsy skirts and gauzy blouses, headband scarves that draped over their shoulders and several necklaces with odd-shaped pendants, greeted them. All over the shop were signs indicating a sale on unicorns.

"We don't have the oddities of other stores here," the one in all purple announced.

As if a part of her, the woman in orange continued, "Our purpose is to help those who wish to transcend to another plane."

Curiosity got to Chelsea. "How do you do that?"

"Most of our customers already have the gift," the purple lady said, narrowing her eyes at Chelsea and then Dylan, as if assessing the possibility in either of them.

"Gift?" Dylan asked in the skeptical tone of an IRS man in the middle of an audit.

"Telekinesis, telepathy."

The lady in orange shook her head. "No crystal balls here."

And no answer she'd hoped for, Chelsea mused while exiting the store with Dylan minutes later.

"Do you think they can talk if the other person isn't around?" he quipped.

"That was strange, wasn't it?" Her voice trailed off as she stared at the next store's window display. Black cloth draped the display window like a curtain to show off a silver pentagram. "Dylan, Aunt Marlin wouldn't go in there," Chelsea said, noting the garlic hanging on the door.

He wasn't too thrilled about doing it himself. He planned to enter only three more stores on the list that Chelsea had compiled. "If I'm not out in five minutes, call someone."

He was back in two.

"Was it strange in there?" Chelsea asked the moment he joined her.

"Some guy dressed like Dracula answered my questions."

"He never saw my aunt, did he?"

"Nope."

Though she'd been certain that type of place wasn't her aunt's style, she felt relief.

"This one looks kind of tame in comparison," Dylan commented, referring to the next store they came to, with its window display of herbs. "Probably a waste of time."

A small, dark shop, its aisles were so narrow they barely allowed enough room for Chelsea to push the stroller through them. Crystals, rocks, bottles of colored liquid, candles and boxes of herbs cluttered the shelves lining the walls.

"Ah, you've come for a love potion," a grandmotherly-looking woman asked, stopping Dylan from following Chelsea further down the aisle.

Dylan cracked a grin. Quite possibly he could use one. Over the woman's shoulder, he watched Chelsea browsing in front of shelves of books. "That's not why we came in. We need—"

"You wish to predict the future," the woman said with deadly seriousness.

Overhearing her, Chelsea shot an amused look back at Dylan. "Actually—"

"You could use hazel twig," she said, seeming lost in her own thoughts as she rounded the counter to reach into a container on a shelf.

"No! No hazel twig," Dylan insisted, halting her action.

She refaced him, her eyes narrowing speculatively.

"No, you don't appear right for that. Tea leaves, perhaps. Or runes."

Chelsea inched Max's stroller closer. "Pardon?"

Dylan rolled his eyes, and behind the woman's back, he stretched out an arm, indicating it was Chelsea's turn to attempt some kind of a sensible conversation with the store owner and get answers to their questions.

"Casting the runes," the woman explained. "Letter symbols of an ancient alphabet."

Dylan stepped away and shifted his attention from a Ouija board to a wall chart of tarot cards identified as the Horoscope Spread.

"Numerology works for beginners," the woman continued.

Too polite to interrupt, Chelsea shook her head, Dylan noted.

"Palm reading is quite a bit more difficult. I hope you didn't have your heart set on that."

"No, we aren't—"

"We have questions to ask," Dylan interrupted while stepping closer.

The woman's friendly smile slipped. "You're police?" she questioned, with a puzzled look at Max.

"No," Chelsea assured her.

The woman sent a disgusted look in Dylan's direction. "You're skeptics, aren't you." She shook her head with disdain. "Many emperors and kings sought the assistance of what they referred to as 'cunning men' to tell their futures."

Chelsea cut in. "I'm trying to locate my aunt. I have a photograph. I thought perhaps you know her."

The woman delivered a cursory glance at the photograph, then did a double-take. "Marlie." Her tone warmed at the nickname she'd said. "You're Marlie's niece?"

"Yes. I'm—"

"She's back," the woman interrupted.

Finally she'd found someone who knew her aunt. "Yes, I'm trying to find her."

"That shouldn't be difficult. She said she came back because of her grandson."

Uneasiness rippled through Chelsea. Had her aunt discussed Max with others because of plans to move him in with her?

"I told her that it's not so easy to raise kids today. But you know her, she's like the Unsinkable Molly Brown. She thinks she can do anything."

A family trait, Dylan mused.

As a bell tinkled above the door, the woman eyed the new customer.

"Do you know where she's staying?" Chelsea asked.

The woman started toward the other customer. "She never said."

Discouraged, Chelsea obeyed Dylan's hand under her elbow, urging her in the direction of the door. "Thank you," she called back before Dylan propelled her outside. She sent him a troubled look. "Oh, Dylan, she wants him."

So do we, Dylan nearly said.

Wrestling with panic, Chelsea gripped his arm.

A need swept over him to protect her, to take all the feelings, imaginary or not, that were agonizing her. Never had he wished for the power to slip inside someone else's skin, bear her pain. "Shh, calm down." He slipped an arm around her shoulder. "You said yourself that she's flighty."

Chelsea's knees felt weaker. "She wants him," she repeated softly, as if afraid to hear her own words.

Upset, while dressing for the gathering at her mother's, Chelsea fought depressing thoughts about her aunt's intentions. It occurred to her that she'd been like an ostrich sticking its head in the sand, or she'd have realized that she was bound to lose Max. If her aunt didn't want him, Dylan might have the right.

At some moment since she'd knocked on his door with Max in her arms, Dylan had begun to bond with Max. She was certain she hadn't misread the love and tenderness he'd shown with Max. If he was Max's father, he would take him with love in his heart. But where she would fit into the picture then was suddenly painfully clear—nowhere. If either her aunt or Dylan chose to keep Max, she would lose.

She'd planned to mask her mood at Richman's gathering, but later that day, when Dylan arrived, he opened his arms to her as if he sensed she needed comfort most.

"It's going to be okay," he soothed. He felt her body go soft against him as though she needed support. The hopelessness in her action stunned him. "Don't give up now."

"I'm not," she assured him, forcing a smile. But she needed more assurances and hoped her mother could give them. "You look nice," she said, to avert conversation away from her worry. Decked out in a dark suit, he represented the kind of man suitable for her by Huntsford standards.

"You look beautiful." The form-fitting white-and-green flowery dress that flowed to her ankles complemented the red in her hair. The soft material ripened his fantasy about what was beneath it.

Sliding her arm around his back, she struggled to lighten her mood. "I'd stay home if I could." She flashed a smile. It was the most genuine smile she'd felt since leaving that store.

Dylan brushed his lips against hers. "Let's go. The sooner we go—"

"The sooner we can leave," she said finishing for him.

"Big bash," Dylan noted while he was pulling onto the circular driveway for a valet to park his car.

Laughter and conversation floated from the house. "No Huntsford ever hosted a little get-together," Chelsea commented. A harpist entertained guests with strains of Bach. People overflowed to the terrace and the inner courtyard gardens. Overhead, a rainbow of colors danced in the crystal chandelier. Determined to keep worried thoughts about her aunt from escalating, Chelsea slipped her hand from Dylan's. "I want to find my mother."

"I'll get a drink." He didn't move until she disappeared into another room. He already wished she was back, he realized, maneuvering his way to the bar.

Predictable as ever, Chelsea's mother was flitting around the kitchen supervising last-minute food preparations. The caterer, a high-energy, thin man, bustled around the counter, but kept returning to one of the kitchen windows. "I don't know what we'll do, Mrs. Huntsford. It looks like rain."

Chelsea stifled a smile as she met her mother's quick glance. "It wouldn't dare," she said.

"Oh, my, but I think it might," the man said in a disgusted tone, then sighed. "And we've already set up tents and tables outside. Sardines. With so many people stuffed in the rooms, they'll feel like sardines."

This time Chelsea did smile. She loved his exaggerations.

Competent and calm under any circumstances, her mother patted his shoulder reassuringly. "André, you mustn't worry so. Everything will be wonderful, as always."

He gave her a grateful look and bent forward to kiss her hand. "And you, marvelous lady, always are a joy and pleasure to work with."

Beaming, her mother turned and whispered to Chelsea, "He's always so pleasant, but such a worrier."

Chelsea hooked her arm with her mother's. "So are you."

Affectionately, her mother touched her hand. "I want everything to be nice."

"It always is," Chelsea assured her. "They should give you an award for perfect hostess."

"Thank you, dear. Are you alone?" She touched a

strand of Chelsea's hair. "You look so pretty this evening."

"Dylan is here." Her mother leveled one of her long, steady stares. Though her mother's hands weren't on her, Chelsea felt her nudge in Dylan's direction. "Guests have arrived." Urging her toward the foyer to avoid further discussion about Dylan, Chelsea steered the conversation to what the store owner had said about her aunt.

Maternal soothing didn't help. Chelsea left her mother with more uneasiness and searched the sea of faces for Dylan. Only he understood her anxiety about Max, she mused. Yet was he burdened by the desperation she felt to keep Max? Did he want him? Despite the closeness between them, he'd never stated what he hoped for concerning Max.

Sidestepping several people loitering in the arched doorway, she was halted by a bridge friend of her mother's. Trapped by the loquacious woman, she nodded agreeably to everything she said.

From across the room, Dylan wound a path to her. The woman's eyes widened as he stepped near.

Chelsea made the expected introduction, then excused herself. Walking away with Dylan, she welcomed the sturdiness of his arm at her waist. "Thank you for rescuing me."

Lightly, he brushed his lips against her temple. "My pleasure." She looked less stressed. "Did you find your mother?"

Chelsea shifted toward him. "Yes. I asked her about Aunt Marlin. She didn't think Aunt Marlin was serious about taking Max."

He looked for doubts in her eyes. If she had them, she hid them well. "Feel better?"

"Oh, Chelsea," a voice sang out. "You must be thrilled," her mother's friend Elizabeth gushed, sidling close to them. "Won't it be wonderful to have a senator in the family?"

"Yes, it will," she said honestly, not because of the distinguished position Richman sought, but because she knew how happy the win would make him.

"You're being signaled," Dylan whispered close to her ear.

Chelsea couldn't ignore her mother's gesture to join her and Richman. But she'd hoped for a little time before the official business, which included speeches. "I wanted to call Tess and check on Max."

Dylan unlaced his fingers from hers. "I'll call."

"I'll give you the phone number."

He kissed her cheek. "Have it."

"You were going to call Tess and check on Max?"

"Could be paternal instinct," he said, with a laugh at himself.

Nothing else needed to be said. Chelsea knew now that he wanted Max, too. He'd become as much a part of his life as hers.

When Dylan disappeared in the library, Chelsea maneuvered herself through the crowd to stand beside her mother. Everyone gathered for the expected speech by Richman's campaign manager. Glasses were raised, a toast made. Richman preened at the applause that followed his brief speech, the first of many he would make.

As people gathered around him with words of political support, Chelsea wandered toward the library to find Dylan. In passing, she caught snatches of conversation regarding endorsements. With all her heart she loved her brother, was pleased for him, happy that he was achieving what he longed for. But the child who'd grown up in this house, and in her brother's shadow, still lingered within her. Restless, she found herself drawn to her father's portrait on the drawing room wall. Tonight he would have been beaming about one of them.

"Chelsea?" Closing the double doors behind her first, Victoria glided in. "Are you still worrying about your aunt?"

That and more, Chelsea could have told her.

"I was thinking about Father."

Her mother linked her arm with Chelsea's. "He would be so proud of both of you."

Perhaps it was the honesty she'd faced over feelings for Dylan that made her feel different. Whatever the reason, she couldn't pretend any longer about what had never existed between her father and her. "He wouldn't have been impressed with what I've done." At best, his feelings for her had been apathetic.

"Chelsea—"

Hurting her was the last thing Chelsea wanted to do, but she couldn't feign a wonderful father-daughter relationship any longer. "Mother, no matter what you say to make this better, it won't work." She spoke with a candor she'd curbed most of her life. "For years, I let you excuse his attitude toward me, but I never believed you.'' She knew now no one could make someone else love her.

Her mother's eyes clouded. ''Why didn't you say something?''

''I knew it made you feel better to believe that I accepted what you'd said.'' Avoiding her mother's eyes, she suggested, ''We should join the guests.''

''They can wait,'' she said firmly.

Chelsea felt a steely grip in the delicate, manicured hand on her forearm. ''It's not important, not really.'' She regretted that she'd started this conversation. ''It's the past.''

''Sometimes the past makes the future unclear. You believed he only had time for Richman, didn't you?''

With a resigned sigh, she spoke without emotion. ''You know that's true.''

Taking a seat on a cushion of the nearby brocade settee, her mother lowered her head. ''I'm sorry, sorry for all the hurt I caused you.''

Chelsea joined her. Knees touching her mother's, she reached for her hand. ''You didn't cause any of it. And I didn't say this to make you feel bad. I'm sorry that I—''

''Hush. I did cause it.'' Anguish colored her voice. ''I did because I never told you the truth.'' A sigh full of agony slipped from her lips. Slowly she raised her face as if making eye contact might be the hardest thing she'd ever done. ''While he was alive, your father insisted I tell no one, but I knew that was wrong. I can't blame only him. I shouldn't have agreed. I knew you had a right to know what I'd done.''

"What you'd done?"

"There was a man, Chelsea. I only saw him a few times. But—"

"A man?" Did she mean she'd had an affair? Though the idea of her mother breaking marriage vows went against all she believed in, why would her parents keep that from her when she'd become an adult? Or had they kept it from everyone? Her father was a prideful man, one who would stiffen if confronted by some family embarrassment. "No one could tell. You seemed so devoted. He seemed so committed."

"With your father, it was an absolute that no one learn about it. And publicly he acted the part, but he never forgave me."

Had she endured a loveless marriage for the sake of the Huntsford name? Chelsea couldn't stop herself from asking. "Did you love the other man?"

Shame paled her mother's face. "He paid attention to me when I needed it."

Chelsea yearned for words of comfort. How well she understood how her father's lack of attention could leave a person wanting.

"There is no easy way to tell you this." Her mother's voice cracked. "The man never knew I was pregnant."

"Pregnant?" Time stopped as a realization began to slowly sweep over her. Still, she asked, "Was there another child?"

Her mother's shoulders sagged. "No. He—he was

your father," she said so softly it came out on a whisper.

Chelsea labored for a breath. "What?"

"Forgive me." Her mother reached out, then yanked her hand back. "I was afraid. Afraid that I'd lose you. That you'd never forgive me if you knew the truth. Believe me. Please, Chelsea, believe this if nothing else. It was me Charles hated, not you."

Nothing was real. Her whole life had been a lie. The father whose love she'd yearned for hadn't been her real one. Anger seeped through her disbelief. "If that were true, why didn't he divorce you?" she challenged.

Tears her mother had held in streaked her cheeks now. "He was prideful. You know that." Her mother's voice caught. "He could be spiteful. He even threatened to fight for both of you. I would have had no one. And he hadn't wanted the scandal. No Huntsford has ever divorced. To separate the family broke some unspoken code. Chelsea—I—" Tears flowed down her cheeks. "Please. Please understand."

Inwardly shaking, Chelsea hugged herself. Too many thoughts raced through her mind. All those years she'd wanted so much for him to offer a token of love. She'd ached with guilt, wondering what she'd done wrong.

"I have no excuse," her mother whispered. "I didn't want to lose my children."

Slowly Chelsea raised her gaze. Yes, for a child, for Max, wouldn't she do anything?

"I should have protected you," her mother barely managed to say in a broken voice. "It's my fault you endured so much, but—" She kept her head bowed. "I'd hoped, prayed he would treat you like his daughter. But he was a cold man. Even with Richman, he had difficulty showing his feelings. Still, I knew how much you loved him. I couldn't understand that he never realized how much love he could have had from you." Inconsolable, her mother sobbed.

How unhappy she must have been, too. Chelsea pressed her lips tightly together to prevent tears. Through all those years, one person, her mother, had always been there for her. How could she blame her for a mistake made years ago, for wanting to stay with her children at any cost? Instead of anger, she longed to ease the torment of someone who'd shown her unquestionable love her whole life. She wished for words to alleviate her mother's shame. None came to mind, so she simply gathered her close.

She shook in Chelsea's arms. "I'd prayed you'd understand—wouldn't hate me."

"Mother, no more."

"A child, any child, is such a blessing."

Chelsea drew a deep breath. Yes, a child was. She knew that because of Max. She knew what her father had never learned. A child didn't have to be your own to be a part of your heart.

"I know you can't really understand why I kept the truth from you."

As her mother drew back, Chelsea closed a hand on her mother's icy one. "I understand what matters most." She touched her mother's soft cheek. "You love me."

"I've always loved you more than life itself."

"I know." Her eyes stinging from unshed tears, Chelsea assured her. "And I love you."

Dylan had kept to himself after he made the phone call to Tess. He'd caught several people looking in his direction. Some had sent looks of approval. Others had turned their faces away as if to veil their gossiping.

With a drink in his hand, he wandered outside. Earlier he'd stopped at Alex's office, made the arrangements with him to set up the trust for Max.

Alex had asked one question. "Why?"

Dylan knew the answer. He loved the boy as much as he loved the woman who'd taught him how to love. Idly, he followed a cobblestone path away from the house. The sound of the party, the buzz of voices and laughter, made him look back. He spotted Chelsea, stepping outside. Her back to him, she hunched her shoulders, as if protecting herself from something invisible. Closing the distance to her, he hesitated a moment. She looked caught up in a world of thoughts. Not knowing what was wrong, he stepped near and bent his head to kiss the side of her neck. She leaned back toward him as if eager for the kiss. "How did you know it was me? It might have been that blustery fellow talking to your brother," he said lightly, to gauge her mood.

"I knew." Emotions too strong to resist pulled at

her. She couldn't hide them from him, but she tried. "Did you talk to Tess?"

Concern for her nagging at him, he turned her to face him. "Tess said Max took two bottles, then went to sleep." A warm breeze tossed her hair, its color lost beneath the night's shadows. Moonlight slanted across her face, made her eyes glimmer. But he felt an unmistakable tenseness in her body. The small of her back seemed to draw forward in some protective instinct. Lightly his mouth closed over hers with a comforting kiss. "You disappeared for quite a while," he murmured.

Chelsea clung to him. She would have liked to share the confusion she felt about the man she'd thought was her father. From what had been lost in the past few minutes, she'd gained the knowledge that her father's lack of love hadn't been her fault. She knew now she would never have pleased him. She knew, too, that love couldn't exist if it wasn't mutual.

Despite more closeness with Dylan than she ever expected, she never forgot that they were together, not because of some undying need for each other, but because Max had come into their lives.

Touching her chin, Dylan raised her face to him. "What's troubling you?"

"I learned something I never knew. It was a shock."

Tenderly, in a way she was becoming familiar with, he framed her face with his hands. "Need to tell someone?"

Talking about any of that wouldn't change anything. "No, I'm fine." No longer was she prone to unconditional faith in people. She'd learned that trust went beyond the heart's desire. What she and Dylan had would change when he received the result of the DNA test. If he wasn't Max's father, he would walk out of her life again. Even if he was, that might happen, and something worse. She would lose to him the child she breathed for. Closing her eyes, she rested her cheek against his, wanting the impossible—to have both of them.

Chapter Thirteen

Sunlight filled the bedroom. Dylan had awakened before dawn. Through the night, he'd felt Chelsea's stirrings, her restlessness. He hadn't slept well, either. Marriage. He'd never considered it before, and now he was anxious to ask the question. And gutless. What if she said no? What if she didn't believe him? With his fingertips, he stroked her hair. "Something happened last night at the party, didn't it?"

Slowly Chelsea raised herself and stared into eyes that were intense and searching, and filled with compassion. She wasn't Charles Estes Huntsford's daughter. Some other man's. That had been her first thought upon awakening. She needed to know his name. In time, if he was alive, she would like to meet him.

No, maybe she wouldn't. Love had flowed between her and her mother, and between her brother and her, but the man she'd thought of as her father had held her at a distance, and that had excluded him from being part of a real family. Even without her real father, she would always be a part of a family.

"Is it a family secret?"

There was no one else she would share that secret with. As if talking to herself, she told him now what her mother had revealed last night.

In the dim light, he could make out the slant of her cheekbones. He'd never known his father. How could he relate to her grief at losing one? With a fingertip, he traced her mouth, felt the warmth of her quiet breaths against his hand. She shouldn't have known a childhood of rejection. Whether or not her father had been bitter about his wife's betrayal, he should have protected the child from his anger. "He never deserved you."

"I know now why he acted the way he did," Chelsea said quietly. "But I'm not a child anymore." She cuddled closer. She was done letting the past control her. She'd made a career for herself. She'd proved she was competent at doing anything she wanted. She smiled as Dylan drew her closer. The gentleness of his lips on her cheek felt soothing. The caress of his hand gave her solace. Shifting, she fastened her mouth on his. With no thought but of the moment, she touched him, heard his groan.

How much time passed escaped him. At the brush of her fingers over his chest, Dylan groped his way back to reality.

More relaxed, Chelsea was tempted to stay in bed

for as long as he wanted, but a glance at the clock roused her. "Are you ready to get up?"

"I was waiting for the smell of coffee first," he teased.

"You were?" Softly she laughed and started to sit up.

Staring at her slim, naked back, he caught her shoulder and pulled her back down. "Maybe it can wait," he murmured in her ear.

"I thought you had a busy day. Aren't we still going to your company picnic this afternoon?"

Dylan grimaced about the mandatory appearance at the picnic. While he was sidetracked by his thoughts, she scurried from bed. An unexpected sense of serenity swept through him. Desperately he wanted to blurt out how much he loved her, that he wanted to marry her. But she deserved better—candlelight and romance. Easing from the bed, he tugged up his pants, then strolled toward the kitchen. "You're still going with me, aren't you?"

Chelsea released the refrigerator door. "It'll take me time to get ready, and you'll be late."

Bracing a shoulder against the doorjamb, he smiled. "I'll wait." Being alone seemed alien now. She was a part of him. She was what he needed in his life.

He took Max from her arms, then grabbed a bottle from the table. "Hey, Max, still hungry?" He'd become an old hand at this. Amazing how much one little person could change someone's life in just weeks. He'd been so footloose before. The only commitment he'd had was to his company. He hadn't been happy, Dylan knew now.

Sitting at the kitchen table, he cradled Max in one arm while he sipped at coffee. From the bedroom, he heard Chelsea humming. Here was real happiness. Maybe he was always meant to be a father because he'd never had one. Maybe everything he'd done without had been because he would get so much later.

"I'm ready," Chelsea said while rushing in from the other room.

His heartbeat skipped. She could have been wearing a sweatsuit and looked wonderful to him. As it was, the peach-colored dress emphasized her pale skin, enriched the color of her hair. "You are amazingly quick."

"A necessity in my business."

"And you are definitely worth waiting for."

Chelsea willed away the start of a blush. "Thank you. Is the dress okay?" she asked, turning in a circle.

"She's awfully pretty, isn't she?" he said conspiratorially in Max's ear.

Chelsea laughed. He made her feel pretty. She knew now so much of what she'd felt about herself had been because of her father's hurtful remarks. Oh, she'd never be as beautiful as a model, but she looked in a mirror now and saw that she wasn't unattractive or as ordinary as she'd once believed. "The two of you will give me a big head if you don't stop."

Standing, Dylan closed the distance to her and took her hand in his.

"You're good for me," she murmured.

"That was my line."

As she laughed, the sound floated on the air, stirring his smile.

Aware they might be even later if she stayed in his arms, Chelsea slipped away to check the diaper bag. "I forgot Max's pacifier." She rushed toward the bedroom, already wondering where she'd put it, and prepared for a search.

They probably would be late, Dylan mused. He didn't care. All he cared about was her and Max. Quite a revelation for a man who'd always viewed himself as a loner. Looking down in response to his beeper, Dylan frowned at the unfamiliar number, then reached for the phone.

The pacifier clutched in her hand, Chelsea stepped in to see Dylan setting down the telephone. Lost in her own thoughts, she hadn't heard it ring. "Who was on the phone?"

"My beeper went off," he said in a flat tone, not looking at her. "I had to make a phone call."

Max blew bubbles from his position on the floor. He looked all right. But something had happened since she'd left. "Dylan?"

"The call was from the lab about the DNA test." He ran a finger over Max's stuffed frog on the end table. "He's not mine."

Not his. The words echoed in her mind. Any expected joy about what that meant to her came and went in the time it took to take a breath. Dylan mattered most. He'd wanted Max. She could see the disappointment in his eyes. How could she feel joy when he was in pain? "I'm sorry. Dylan, I'm sorry." She approached him slowly. "You were beginning to hope he was yours, weren't you?"

He shrugged a shoulder and wandered to the window before she reached him. He should feel relieved. He could get his life back to normal now. But he felt so damn empty. He felt as if something was gone in the vicinity of his heart.

Come on, Marek. So he wasn't Max's father. He should have known Max wasn't his. He'd been a loner most of his life. Being around Chelsea and the boy had messed up his mind. Because of them, he'd begun to think, hell, to dream about a family of his own. Dumb thinking. "I need to go to the office."

"What about the picnic?"

He didn't give a damn about it.

She caught his shrug. Never had someone's pain been so visible. *Don't go.* She wanted to tell him that she understood. She wanted to give him some solace. Chelsea moved quickly, aching to touch him, stop him. But he was already opening the door, preparing to shut her out. Why had she expected differently? They'd made love, but he didn't love her. She'd thought when he'd shared his past with her that she might mean something more to him. There were the foolish dreams again. *Stupid, Chelsea. You never learn.*

Dylan halted at the door. Why did love for anyone always hurt? How could he know he would feel so much pain losing that little boy? And why the hell was he leaving? The one person he needed most at this moment was Chelsea. Slowly he closed the door, then turned to face her.

Chelsea's heart tugged. He looked so sad.

"I'm sorry. I've gotten so used to dealing with everything by myself that I—well, I'm sorry."

Chelsea nodded understandingly. A thread of hope slowly moved through her.

"It hurts," he admitted.

Chelsea caught his hand. She wanted to give him more, but wasn't sure how much he'd accept from her.

"You were right. I wanted him." He gave her a slim smile. "So if I'm not his father, then Alan obviously was."

Chelsea nodded. "I still can't prove that, but I doubt if paternity would be a problem now."

"That's good." Because he needed to touch her, needed the closeness with her, he brushed his knuckles across her cheek. "He should be with you," he said softly, because he believed that.

Chelsea stepped in to the arms opened for her as pleasurable warmth snuck up on her. So did the realization she'd blocked minutes ago. If her aunt behaved as Chelsea expected and didn't want to raise Max, then she could. That sweet little baby who already owned her heart could be hers.

The picnic was in full swing by the time they arrived. Exchanging greetings as he ushered Chelsea toward one picnic table, Dylan caught the discreet reactions of raised eyebrows, the buzz of whispers. Within the company, he'd been considered too eligible of a bachelor not to be married. The sight of him holding a baby sent tongues wagging. He didn't care.

He'd found the woman, the family he'd never had. The whole world could know that now. "It's warm today," he said, guiding her in the direction of company executives and their wives. "Is it too warm for Max?"

Chelsea glanced around at the park with its abundance of trees. "There's plenty of shade."

"Okay, let's make the expected stop over there, and then we'll find a tree to sit under."

With Max in her arms, she settled on the bench while Dylan left to get them something to drink. She'd noted that after Dylan's introduction, beneath polite hellos, several women had critically given her a once-over. In their eyes, she didn't suit Dylan. Too plain. Even with her new haircut and the peach sundress Tess had convinced her to buy, did they believe that she lacked the charisma and sophistication someone like Dylan should choose?

"Some couples do that," one woman at the table was saying disapprovingly in response to another woman's distressed conversation about her daughter. "They never marry. Just keep living together."

Chelsea felt the woman's eyes boring into her. She and Dylan had definitely inspired a lot of gossip, she decided.

"How does that spot look?" Dylan asked, appearing at her side in time to prevent the woman from questioning her.

Chelsea eyed the huge oak tree he'd gestured at. "Looks wonderful," she said with a brighter-than-natural smile for the benefit of watchful eyes.

Together, they spread a blanket, then Dylan wandered away to get them food. He'd been to half a dozen of these picnics and had never felt comfortable, until today. Returning to her, he set a plate with chicken in front of her, then dropped on the blanket beside her. "This looked good."

Concerned for him, Chelsea gave the plate of barbecued food a cursory glance. Around them, employees and their families indulged in the free food, kids scurried around the park. And stares came her way.

She waited only until she and Dylan were driving toward home later to clue him in on what she'd sensed had been happening. He needed to prepare himself for what might be a problem. "Dylan, the ladies were talking."

He made a final turn down her street. "About what?"

"Us. Some of them have definite ideas about marriage. Did anyone ask you if Max was yours?"

"Yeah." He wheeled onto her driveway. Flicking off the ignition, he glanced her way and smiled at the troubled frown etching a line between her brows.

Chelsea inclined her head. He didn't look the least bit concerned. "What did you say?"

"He could be." To him, that was true. Even if he wasn't Max's biological parent, he'd begun to feel like his father.

"Dylan!"

She looked so astonished he couldn't help smiling. "Do you realize what they're thinking?"

"I don't care."

Puzzled by his cavalier attitude, she thought he needed to reconsider.

"Don't be so uptight about it," Dylan suggested while he carried Max in the house.

Chelsea followed him in. She slipped off her shoes, then rinsed empty formula bottles while Dylan settled Max in his crib. "You need to clarify what you meant," she said when Dylan ambled from the bedroom.

"Or marry you." There, he'd said it. His heart pounded. This wasn't the way he'd planned to ask her, but holding the words in proved impossible. Though he needed to pick the right moment, all morning he'd wanted to blurt out his feelings to her. He wondered if after all he'd said before about no commitment, no marriage, she might need some heavy-duty convincing to believe him. "I want to marry you."

Leaning against the kitchen counter, she released a staggered breath. "Marry?" Even as the word rocked her, yes was in her head and her heart. A myriad of emotions and thoughts swamped her. Marriage. He'd never wanted marriage before. Why now? "Are you asking to stop the gossip?"

His private life was his business. "No, I could care less what they think." At her silence, he rolled a shoulder tightening with tension. "Aren't you going to say anything?"

She'd known he might hurt her again, but in her wildest imaginings, she'd never foreseen him asking her to marry him, offering her the one thing she wanted most.

"What's the problem?"

"I never expected you to ask me that."

He wanted to push for her answer. He wanted to tell her that he wasn't the same man anymore. "All you have to do is say yes." He wanted to beg her. How could he explain the love he'd just learned how to feel for her?

How simple he made that sound. At what cost to her heart? she wanted to ask him.

Dylan's stomach constricted. He should have waited, but he'd never said those words to another woman, never had felt so filled with love that it consumed him. If she loved him, why hadn't she said yes? He thought she wanted this. Wasn't that why he'd walked away the first time? There was a lot he wanted to say, but how could he explain what he still didn't totally understand himself?

Desperately, Chelsea longed to accept whatever he said, grab what he offered. But how could she? He'd always insisted on no promises. Why this sudden turnaround? How could she feel joy, believe in them, when he'd never told her he loved her? So why? she wondered again. Why did he want to marry her?

It had nothing to do with them, she realized in that instant. It was all about Max. "I don't understand you." That wasn't entirely true. She understood him too well. *I wanted him,* Dylan had said about Max. He'd meant forever. Now, because he wasn't Max's father, did he believe that the only way he could have Max was by adopting him with her? Was that the reason he really wanted to marry her? "I can't marry you. This isn't about you and me. I know that." No matter how much she loved him, she had to refuse.

"It's about Max. I've seen how much you love him. You don't want to give him up."

To be anything except honest with her never entered his mind. "No, I don't."

"But he's not yours." Pride swelled within her. Not even for Max could she be second best again. "So to get him, you're making yourself do something that I know you never wanted to do."

He felt a catch in his chest. Had he done this to her? Made this sweet, loving woman so distrustful? God forgive him. "Wait a minute," he insisted.

Chelsea steeled herself to any argument he offered. She couldn't, wouldn't ever allow herself to feel unloved again. All or nothing. She wouldn't settle for less. She needed to be cherished.

"Is this all about what happened before?"

Her eyes locked with his. She supposed it was. He'd left her before for someone else. As wonderful as the time with him had been, he'd never said he loved her. Deliberately, she moved away, so the coffee table was between them. If he touched her, she wasn't certain she wouldn't weaken. "This is about now, about you suddenly wanting marriage." He'd come into her life, not out of some desperate need to be with her, but because of Max. "What reason could you have for wanting it now?" Did he think she was so foolish that she didn't know what he was doing? He'd offered marriage only after he'd known he'd lost Max. "Why not yesterday or the day before? There is only one reason—Max."

"Do you think I'd hurt you like that?" Dylan demanded, his patience thinning. "Everything has changed.'' With his step forward, she recoiled from his touch.

"Nothing has changed."

He heard a lot of hurt in her voice, hurt that he'd caused. He'd never meant to hurt her. Before, he'd wanted to protect her. Now he simply wanted to love her. "Listen—" He paused and shot a look of disgust in the direction of the phone, which was ringing. Frustrated, he whipped away. Was his timing so off? What could he say? He gave himself a quick pep talk. If all the love songs were right, she would believe him.

"Yes, I understand," Chelsea said to the caller.

It wasn't her words but the tightness in her voice that alerted Dylan.

Her back straight, she looked as if she were ready to face a firing squad. "Chelsea, what's wrong?"

"We both lose." She choked on the words. "It was Aunt Marlin. She wants me to bring Max to her tomorrow morning." Her voice broke. "Dylan, she wants him. She wants him." Pain so physical she wanted to curl up with it took over. She struggled to blink back the tears smarting her eyes. "She won't let me have Max."

Dylan reached out to draw her into his arms. This was all wrong. Max was meant to be with her.

Before he was a step from her, Chelsea pulled back. She wanted to rush into his arms, lean on someone. It took more strength than she thought she possessed to keep away from him. "Don't."

He didn't move. She'd acted as if his touch would burn her. Trying to ignore his own hurt, he held his arms out, palms up in an appeal. "Chelsea, let me help."

"Leave," she insisted, wanting to be alone, to hold Max to her. Weep. "Go. Just go." Her emotions raw, she hurried into Max's bedroom. She couldn't think about anything else, or anyone. She wanted the baby she desperately loved.

As she reached for Max, she heard her front door close. Filled with an agony that promised to tear her open, she tightened her arms around him. She rocked with a pain that she thought she would die from. She couldn't let Max go; she couldn't. Bending over, she pressed her face close to Max's head, and wept.

Chapter Fourteen

Dylan had a lousy night. Cursing, he'd entered his apartment and dropped to the closest chair with a Scotch in his hand. The thought of a future without Chelsea and Max was unbearable. After drinking too many Scotches, he fell asleep on the chair in the living room.

At daybreak, he awoke with a throbbing head and a sore back. He awoke thinking of her, and for the first time in his life, he knew the agony of missing, of caring about not one but two people.

The emptiness inside him intensifying, he padded toward the bathroom to shower. His steps slowed outside the guest bedroom. Propped in a corner was Max's Portacrib. Anger born of frustration whipped through him. He should have taken it back to her weeks ago. Now what did he do with it, with any of Max's things?

Ambling into the room, he paused and tapped a finger at the roly-poly ball he'd never returned. Damn, this was wrong. Holding the ball, he remembered Max's tiny fingers nudging it. He belonged with Chelsea. With them.

His back to a wall, he slid down to the floor. Legs bent, he rotated the ball in his hands. He'd lost so much, so damn much. And they'd given him so much.

Wasn't this kind of pain what he'd wanted to avoid? Give too much of yourself, and you hurt. He'd learned that lesson early in life. And he'd forgotten it because of one small baby, because of one woman who might never want him again. And because of love. He loved both of them beyond what he thought possible.

So now what? Somehow he had to figure a way to have a second chance with Chelsea. Max was another story. The baby they both wanted wasn't theirs.

He stepped into the shower and let the water spray over him. How was Chelsea handling everything? He should be with her. Two people were grieving for the same reason. They should be able to comfort each other.

He shouldn't have left her. That was his first mistake.

He should go with her to her aunt's. He was good at negotiating. He might even convince her aunt that Max would be better with them. All he had to do first was convince Chelsea to believe in *them.*

Of course, she wouldn't believe anything else he

said, especially now. He'd waited too long. He should have asked her to marry him before learning that he wasn't Max's father. Then she would have believed him. But now she believed this was all about Max. Why had she? Why hadn't he been able to win her trust? Because she believed he hadn't wanted anything permanent? People change; he'd changed.

Dylan shut off the water. Dense. He was truly dense. He'd told her everything except that he loved her. He'd never told her that he loved her.

It took no more than fifteen minutes to dress and drive to her house. What he never expected was no answer. He jumped back in the car and dug in his wallet for Tess's phone number. He counted four rings before Tess answered. "It's Dylan," he said, answering her greeting.

Silence ensued, then a grumpy response that indicated Chelsea had shared her feelings about him with her friend. "Chelsea isn't here."

"Where is she?"

"I don't know."

"Oh, come on, Tess. You have scheduled jobs. Where is she this morning? I have to talk to her."

"Dylan, she's kind of upset."

He sensed an ally. "I know she's upset." What woman wouldn't be? She was about to lose the baby she loved this morning. "Tell me, Tess."

"She's probably at the park. Walking a dog. The Schmidt's sheepdog—Waldo."

"What park?" he asked impatiently, then remembered their previous walk with that dog.

"It's the one that's a couple of blocks from me. The Schmidts are neighbors of—"

"Okay. So she'll be in that park?"

"Yes, but—"

"Don't you dare tell her I'm coming," he insisted, worried Chelsea would take off if she knew.

"I won't. I promise."

Patiently, Chelsea waited for Waldo to finish sniffing his sixth tree in the last three minutes. "Come on, Waldo." This morning's weather report had made her stop at Tess's apartment and leave Max with her. The rain had stopped before she'd picked up Waldo, but the idea of pushing Max around the park in bad weather was unthinkable. *Max.* Her heart tightened. How could she let him go?

"That dog still needs training."

In response to Dylan's voice, Chelsea snapped around. Her pulse pounding, she couldn't ignore the love yearning within her, the desire to fall into his arms. Her throat felt so dry she could barely swallow.

"Where's Max?" Was he imagining it, or had he seen longing in her eyes?

"With Tess." It hurt to even talk about him. Tears smarted her eyes, threatening again, as they had all morning.

Dylan's heart twisted for her. What could he say to comfort her? "When are you going to see Marlin?"

"After I take Waldo home."

With a turn of her shoulders away from him, an ache skittered through Dylan. Only one thought crossed his mind. He wasn't letting her go. He'd spent his whole life looking for someone like her. "We need to talk."

She really couldn't handle this now. "About what?"

He'd spent years dodging too much emotion, convincing himself he didn't believe in love. But he did. Couldn't she see he ached for her, would die for her? "You need to know what happened before, why I walked away from you. It wasn't you. It was me. I couldn't give more than a physical commitment to you, and I knew you'd want everything; Lauren didn't. But I'm not the same man anymore."

He *was* different, Chelsea knew. He'd learned to feel for a little boy. He'd learned how to love, but that didn't change what she'd accepted from the beginning. "I wouldn't ever marry someone who doesn't love me."

"Who said I don't? What if we both agree that I've been stupid?" He watched her closely. Her chin wasn't angled away anymore. Some of the tension had eased from her shoulders, relaxing them. "Chelsea, years ago, you were too much the type of woman I did want. I didn't want to hurt you. I knew you'd have expected more then." He wasn't sure what to say to convince her. "And I ran. I ran because getting too close to anyone hurt. I learned that early in life. I think—" Honesty required courage, he decided. "I think I knew I could fall in love with you."

Her heart hammered so hard she thought it would burst through her chest. "Love?"

"You and I belong together." His voice softened

slightly. "Max, too. But as much as I wish I could give you what you want most, I can't get Max for you."

Her throat tightened at the torment she heard in his voice.

"I love you. I don't want to live without you."

Chelsea stilled. He'd said it. He'd really said that he loved her even though he knew she had to take Max to Marlin. There was no reason to say that unless— Stunned, she could hardly breathe. What had she done? He'd been telling the truth. He wanted her, really wanted her. "You really love me."

The astonishment on her face made him want to crush her to him. "Just answer one question. Do you love me? I know I'm not easy to love but..."

Chelsea dared a step closer. "Oh, but you are."

Tenderly he touched her cheek. "I want you. I want to marry you. I'm sorry it took so long for me to realize how much I needed you. Will you marry me?"

"I think it's what I've always wanted," Chelsea murmured against his lips.

But rather than deepening the kiss, he pulled back. "There's something else. And no argument about this. Okay? We'll have our own kids, but—"

"Will we?" She smiled, and brushed a tear from her cheek. "Do you want children?"

"As much as you do. But Max. I've thought a lot about him. Why can't we be a part of his life? Marlin can't raise him alone. She'll need help. Us. We can take him places. Go with him on his first day of school. He is a part of us now, isn't he?"

Max was. She nearly cried from the myriad of emotions rushing through her. He wanted everything she did.

"I'm going with you to see Marlin," Dylan insisted. "We'll convince her." He held her even tighter to him. "We won't let him go."

"I've tried to understand why she'd want him," Chelsea said when he drove to the address her aunt had given her. "She's only seen him once since his birth. She's been gallivanting around the world since Lauren's death, consoling herself in adventure. A baby would slow her down. Why doesn't she realize that?"

Dylan wished for words, any words to ease her mind. In the rearview mirror, he watched Max, sleeping peacefully. He would give up everything he'd worked hard for to just keep him.

Instead of her aunt, a birdlike woman with a lopsided gray bun opened the door. "Marlin's been living with me," she informed them as a greeting. "She's intent on learning scrying. Crystal-gazing." The woman flung an ostrich feather wrap over her shoulder that trailed down her back to the start of her loose-fitting jeans. "I have a shew-stone."

"Shew-stone?" Chelsea was mentally lost. Emotionally exhausted, she simply wanted to see her aunt. The longer she held Max in her arms, the more she was tempted to whip around and run with him.

"I've forgotten. Marlin said her family wasn't aware."

Chelsea assumed that *aware* meant believers in fortune-telling.

"A shew-stone is often made from a cabochon-cut beryl stone." She flung her hand to the side, to direct their attention to her living room, where a crystal was mounted within a frame of polished ivory. Some kind of writing had been inscribed in gold letters. It sat upon a glass pedestal that rested on a circular table.

"Your aunt is in there," she said, pointing a finger to an adjacent dimly lit room. "Be quiet. She's developing her creative visual imagination."

Chelsea nodded and held Max tighter as she stepped past her and into the house. Incense that made her feel dizzy permeated the rooms.

"Not you," the woman said to Dylan. A head smaller than him, she blocked his path to prevent him from entering. "Only she comes in. Marlin didn't say anything about *him* visiting."

Dylan tightened a rein on his emotions. He couldn't afford to lose his temper with the woman.

Chelsea watched his lips set in a stubborn line, and sent him a silent plea with a look.

Against his good judgment, Dylan nodded agreeably.

"Your aura is awful. Purple," the woman quipped at him, turning up her top lip.

Dylan shoved a hand into his pocket. He didn't give a damn about his aura. All he cared about was the woman he loved, the child he loved. If Marlin took Max, she would tear out the heart of the sweetest woman he knew.

* * *

Chelsea found her aunt seated at a table, her eyes fixed on a glass of water. Instinctively she drew Max tighter to her breast. If Max lived with her aunt, would she hear him if he was crying? Would she remember to feed him? What about when he got older? Would she be too involved in her own world to worry about his grades, go to a baseball game with him, listen to him and learn what he thought, what he felt?

"Chelsea." Eyes fixed on the glass, her aunt spoke without looking back at her. "Come in, dear. Sit down."

Chelsea moved to the settee opposite her.

"Oh, my," she said, staring again at the water. "Green clouds. Hmmm."

Chelsea held Max on her lap and pressed her lips to the top of his head. Oh, please, stop this. Everything is nonsense except what I have to say to you. It's the most important question I've ever asked in my life.

"That usually indicates coming happiness." Her eyes darted to Chelsea. "Have you had problems in your love life? I know you tended not to get as involved as often as Lauren did. My sweet girl always had orange clouds. Difficulties ahead, you know. Have you?"

Chelsea released a huge sigh. "In a way."

"No more." She waved her hand horizontally. "Green clouds mean happiness in your emotional life." She stared into the water again. "If I had more time, because you see, time is needed, then I—well, my mind's eye would allow me to see images. Symbolic expressions. Maybe even a heart with initials in it.''

Stop this, Chelsea wanted to scream. She tempered the urge to yell. She couldn't afford to alienate her. ''This is scrying?''

''Yes, it's quite an old method of seeing into the future. I met this wonderful white witch. Well, you know I've always sworn by ancient healers.'' Her voice trailed off as the other woman appeared at the doorway.

''That man's still waiting.''

Puzzlement deepened the lines in her aunt's face.

''Dylan,'' Chelsea informed her, watching the woman pad away in her hot pink slipper socks.

''Has he learned if he's Maximillian's father?''

''He's not.''

''Ah.'' Blue eyes so like Chelsea's mother's widened. ''So Alan was. Yet Dylan is here with you. He loves you, doesn't he?''

With no hesitation, Chelsea answered, ''Yes.''

''I always knew he did. The clouds told me. Even when he was seeing Lauren, I knew. She wouldn't listen to me. She was always headstrong. I suppose she found a way to temporarily distract him from you. But I knew he would come back.''

Chelsea waited for her to stop rambling. ''About Max.'' On edge, she drew Max into the crook of her arm, aware her aunt hadn't displayed any immediate interest in him. Poor Max. My sweet baby. What will your life be like?

Her aunt's eyes finally focused on Max. "He is quite adorable, isn't he?" Briefly, sadness flickered in her eyes. "My Lauren was a beautiful baby, too." She zeroed in on Chelsea. "I can see you adore him," she said, and for a second, Chelsea caught a glimpse of the kind-hearted aunt who used to pat her head and sneak her a piece of candy when she came to visit. "But who wouldn't? He is so sweet, isn't he?"

Her heart twisting, Chelsea longed for a way to stop this moment. She couldn't let Max go. "He's wonderful." *I love him.* "Aunt Marlin, I would have adopted him. We want to adopt him."

"Adopt?" A seriousness swept over her face, bunching her brows. "I never considered that until your mother mentioned it to me this morning."

Chelsea held her breath and said a special thank-you for a woman who understood what loving a child meant, who'd sacrificed everything for her children's sake.

"She pointed out that you would be a wonderful mother. Everyone always said you had strong maternal instincts," her aunt added, her voice light and breezy again. "You always were bringing home stray animals. You drove my sister crazy." She released a little laugh, then turned her attention back to Max. "Seeing him again meant so much to me."

Chelsea's stomach knotted as hope sprang alive within her.

Dylan thought he would go mad waiting. Was this what fathers did when they were forced to pass time in hospital waiting rooms? He couldn't stand another minute. What was happening in there? Was Chelsea in tears? Was Max wailing? He swore softly and was reaching for the door handle when the door opened. Dylan felt his insides clench. Max wasn't in her arms. "Chelsea?"

She raised her face toward him. "Oh, Dylan."

Light shone in her eyes. Her face glowed. As she turned away, he saw Marlin, holding Max. As if in slow motion, he watched her transfer Max to Chelsea's arms.

"You take good care of him. Both of you," Marlin said in a choked voice.

Chelsea recalled a scraped knee, and this woman rocking her, soothing a six-year-old's tears. "His grandmother will visit often."

Tears streaming her cheeks, Marlin smiled. "Oh, yes."

No words could convey the emotion swarming in on Chelsea. She leaned forward and kissed her aunt's cheek. "Thank you."

"No, thank you." She sniffed and dabbed fingertips at her cheeks. "Thank you for loving him so much."

Dylan said nothing, was afraid to say anything. With Max cradled against her, Chelsea stepped outside and fell into his arms. "Dylan, he's ours. Max is ours."

Seconds ticked by while her words settled in. He darted a look at Max, then back at her. "She's really letting you have him?"

Hearing a noticeable roughness in his voice, she blinked back tears of happiness. "*We* have him."

"We—"

Chelsea saw exhilaration in his eyes. "She was very cooperative when I said I had something for her to sign. She said Max was much better off with us than her. She travels so much."

Dylan swallowed against the tightening in his throat, and gave thanks that the woman finally had a logical thought.

"She's busy, she said. With the recent Harmonic Convergence, she feels compelled to live in Guatemala and study Mayan writings."

Dylan didn't care if she went to Timbuktu. Needing to feel the warmth of Max's small body, he took him from Chelsea.

Joy humming through her, Chelsea watched as Dylan lovingly embraced Max and kissed his forehead. "Aunt Marlin signed the papers for us to adopt him."

Slipping his other arm around her waist, Dylan wondered how one man could receive so much. He had the family he'd never had, something he'd wished for so many years ago. A wish he'd foolishly abandoned until this woman, and one little boy, had come into his life. "I thought I'd go crazy out here. I felt like an expectant father."

Chelsea laughed. In the past he'd smiled, but never had she seen such peace in his face until now. "We have a son," she said, smiling while tears streaked her cheeks.

Dylan brought her closer. "It's a great start."

Angling a look up again, she saw the love she'd always longed for. Certainty about them rocketed through her. With a palm, she caressed his cheek. She could have lost both of them. Instead, she had everything she'd ever wanted.

* * * * *

Take 2 bestselling love stories FREE

Plus get a FREE surprise gift!

Special Limited-Time Offer

Mail to Silhouette Reader Service™

> 3010 Walden Avenue
> P.O. Box 1867
> Buffalo, N.Y. 14240-1867

YES! Please send me 2 free Silhouette Special Edition® novels and my free surprise gift. Then send me 6 brand-new novels every month, which I will receive months before they appear in bookstores. Bill me at the low price of $3.57 each plus 25¢ delivery and applicable sales tax, if any.* That's the complete price, and a saving of over 10% off the cover prices—quite a bargain! I understand that accepting the books and gift places me under no obligation ever to buy any books. I can always return a shipment and cancel at any time. Even if I never buy another book from Silhouette, the 2 free books and the surprise gift are mine to keep forever.

235 SEN CH7W

Name	(PLEASE PRINT)	
Address	Apt. No.	
City	State	Zip

This offer is limited to one order per household and not valid to present Silhouette Special Edition® subscribers. *Terms and prices are subject to change without notice. Sales tax applicable in N.Y.

USPED-98 ©1990 Harlequin Enterprises Limited

Silhouette ® SPECIAL EDITION ®

Newfound sisters Bliss, Tiffany and Katie
learn more about family and true love
than they *ever* expected.

A new miniseries by

LISA JACKSON

A FAMILY KIND OF GUY (SE#1191) August 1998
Bliss Cawthorne wanted nothing to do with ex-flame
Mason Lafferty, the cowboy who had destroyed her
dreams of being his bride. Could Bliss withstand his irresistible charm—the second time around?

A FAMILY KIND OF GAL (SE#1207) November 1998
How could widowed single mother Tiffany Santini be
attracted to her sexy brother-in-law, J.D.? Especially
since J.D. was hiding something that could destroy the
love she had just found in his arms....

And watch for the conclusion of this series in
early 1999 with Katie Kinkaid's story in
A FAMILY KIND OF WEDDING.

Available at your favorite retail outlet. Only from

#1195 EVERY COWGIRL'S DREAM—Arlene James
That Special Woman!
Feisty cowgirl Kara Detmeyer could handle just about anything—except the hard-edged stockman escorting her through a dangerous cattle drive. Rye Wagner had stubbornly insisted he'd never settle down again, but a daring Kara had *every* intention of roping in the man of her dreams!

#1196 A HERO FOR SOPHIE JONES—Christine Rimmer
The Jones Gang
Vowing to reclaim his father's lost land, ruthless Sinclair Riker embarked on the heartless seduction of beguiling Sophie B. Jones. But Sophie's sweet, intoxicating kisses had cast a magical spell over him—and he ached to do right by her. Could love transform Sin into Sophie's saint?

#1197 THE MAIL-ORDER MIX-UP—Pamela Toth
Winchester Brides
Travis Winchester fought an irresistible attraction to his missing brother's mail-order bride. Even though he didn't trust Rory Mancini one bit, he married the jilted city gal after taking her under his wing—and into his bed. But he couldn't stop wonderin' if Rory truly loved her *unintended* groom....

#1198 THE COWBOY TAKES A WIFE—Lois Faye Dyer
Sassy CeCe Hawkins was forever bound to her late husband's half brother, Zach Colby. Not only was her unborn baby heir to the Montana ranch Zach desperately coveted—and half-owned—but a forbidden passion for this lonesome, tight-lipped cowboy left her longing for a lifetime of lovin' in his arms.

#1199 STRANDED ON THE RANCH—Pat Warren
When sheltered Kari Sinclair fled her overprotective father, she found herself snowbound with oh-so-sexy rancher Dillon Tracy. Playing house together would be a cinch, right? Wrong! For Kari's fantasies of happily-ever-after could go up in flames if Dillon learned her true identity!

#1200 OLDER, WISER...PREGNANT—Marilyn Pappano
Once upon a time, tempting teenager Laurel Cameron had brought Beau Walker to his knees. Then, she'd lit out of town and left Beau one angry—and bitter—man. Now she was back—pregnant, alone, yearning for a second chance together. Could Beau forgive the past...and learn to love another man's child?